'AWAKENING'

(THE VITH ELEMENT SERIES)

BY

ADELE ROSE

Congratulations

Adele Rose

'Awakening'

By Adele Rose

Copyright © 2016 by Adele Rose

All rights reserved.

This book is a work of fiction. All characters and events in this publication, other than those clearly in the public domain, are fictitious and any resemblance to real persons, living or dead, is purely coincidental. This book may not be re-sold or given away to other people. If you would like to share this book with another person, please purchase an additional copy for each recipient. If you're reading this book and did not purchase it, or it was not purchased for your use only, then please return to the retailer and purchase your own copy. No part of this publication may be reproduced, distributed or transmitted in any form, including electrical or mechanical means, without written permission from the author. However, short quotations may be used in book reviews. Thank you for respecting the hard work of this author.

Book and Cover Design by Adele Rose

First Edition: August 2016

Books by Adele Rose:

The VIth Element Series

Book One: 'Awakening'
Book Two: 'Possession'
Book Three: 'Shattered'
Book Four: 'Torn'

The Devil's Secret Trilogy

Book One: 'Damned'

'One person on their own may be able to save the world. But a team of friends, all working together, have a much greater chance of succeeding...providing that no-one succumbs to evil.'

For my Mum

X Ever since I was born, you have inspired me to live my life to the fullest, achieve my dreams, be my own unique person and aim high. Words cannot describe how much I love you. X

PROLOGUE

Vladimir Alcaeus was, for the first time in his extraordinarily long life, tired. As he walked along the ancient, candle-lit hallways, he sighed, overcome with a sudden weariness. He just wasn't as young as he once was and now, much to his frustration, he was finding each and every day exhausting, despite his remarkable talents and incredible mind.

Stopping temporarily outside the ornate wooden doors before him, to catch his breath, he tightened his flowing cloak more closely around his body. It had gradually been getting colder by the second, as if all the warmth was being sucked out of the atmosphere. It also seemed that the dark, once his comforting friend, was now steadily becoming threatening, filled with shadows half glimpsed and that lurked just out of sight. This could only mean one thing...
Mortimer had re-awoken.

Vladimir Alcaeus shivered even more at the thought of such a foe and clung to the cold doors for support. He had once stopped Mortimer many, many moons ago in an almighty battle – a battle that had changed the course of history forever. That memory haunted him the most.
Vladimir lost himself in a flashback.

*

Mortimer towered over Vladimir, his mouth pulled back in a delighted snarl of victory. His eyes were deadly and dazzling and his ebony hair, normally smooth, was now untameable. As Vladimir lay there, amongst the dirt and debris, he realised that his nemesis was surrounded by both the living and the dead. They stood there, awaiting their master's call. They stood there, awaiting their master's signal. They were his loyal soldiers...ever patient...ever faithful.

Suddenly, he felt something gloopy trickle down the side of his face. One of the dead had spat on him, marking him...mocking him. Vladimir felt rage well up within his chest. And yet, he was too weak to respond. It was pitiful, really. His robes were torn and bloody and he had shrivelled within himself, almost like a snail reseeding into its home. He felt weak. He felt feeble.
He felt crushed.
"You can't win now." Mortimer laughed coldly, his eyes flashing with numerous emotions. "I've got you just where I want you and finally," he paused dramatically, before continuing. "I shall have my revenge and you shall get what you deserve!"

It was then that Mortimer lashed out, kicking him repeatedly until he was almost unrecognisable. Vladimir shuddered with every blow. His head hurt. His feet hurt. His chest hurt. All in all, he was exhausted. Something stroked his face and his eyes lulled. Was that death touching him? Was that death calling him...calling him into an eternal slumber?
"No." Vladimir shocked himself with how fierce his response had been. He spat out blood through gritted teeth, defying both death and Mortimer. One of his eyes was practically swollen shut. "No. You're wrong."

Wincing, slowly, ever so slowly, he found the ability to stand.
It was a miracle.
"I'm sorry you feel the way you do." He added, hoping that the sincerity was there in his gaze. His heart thudded like nothing on Earth. "And I'm sorry for what I've d —"
"SORRY WON'T SAVE YOU NOW!" Mortimer's voice resonated around the battlefield, magnified a million times. "SORRY WILL NEVER SAVE YOU...NOT AFTER WHAT YOU'VE COST ME."

As he stood there, Vladimir could have sworn that he saw the tiniest of drops appear within Mortimer's eyes. However, they were gone almost as quickly as they had appeared. The blow, both physical and emotional, hit him like a bullet to the chest. Vladimir fell winded to the ground, his body wracked with further pain.

"ENOUGH." Mortimer snarled. "I'VE HAD ENOUGH!" Like a stealthy panther, he walked towards Vladimir, his teeth bared. "YOUR TIME'S UP AND MY TIME'S BEGUN."

And so it came to this final moment.

Vladimir was on his knees and Mortimer was almost upon him. Only one could win.

Who would it be?

Gathering up the last of his strength, Vladimir searched deep within himself, finding his waning powers. With a roar of defiance, Vladimir projected his powers onto his enemy. In his eyes, a hardness gleamed. Behind that hardness, seen and known only to Vladimir himself, was remorse and bitterness.

Vladimir's powers hit Mortimer by surprise. He stumbled back, his feet nearly giving way. His followers tittered in shock and alarm, some even reaching out to help their master.

Mortimer furiously waved them away.

A few seconds past – seconds that seemed like forever. It was in these precious few seconds that all held their breath and Mortimer looked down, to assess the damage. Nothing. He was fine, apart from a little bruised. Realising this, Mortimer laughed. He laughed so hard that the sky above them turned black, filling with stormy clouds. He laughed so hard that hot, fiery tears fell from his eyes. He laughed so hard that the ground shuddered, threatening to tear apart. Then, out of the darkness, came a glimmer of light. It grew and grew until Mortimer, crying out, acknowledged where the light was coming from.

It was coming from his chest.

A look of blind panic swiftly filled Mortimer's eyes, before this emotion was claimed by fury and fear.
"NO." He screeched, watching his world crumble, as did his dead companions. "NO. THIS CAN'T BE HAPPENING. IT CAN'T -"
All was to no avail.

Eyes shrivelled. Nose shrivelled. Lips shrivelled, until Mortimer became a glowing beacon in the night. Subsequently, Mortimer fell to the ground, like a charred rock.

*

Vladimir returned to the present. He recalled how he had watched Mortimer's living followers disappear that day, shortly after witnessing the fall of their master. They had scuttled away like spiders. They had seemed to slink into the shadows, hiding and hoping. Vladimir also acknowledged that, after defeating his enemy, he had barely escaped with his life. He had been plagued by endless months of evil, tortured nightmares. In due course, Vladimir had travelled to the furthest dimension known to entomb Mortimer in various, impenetrable barriers. Clearly, the barriers hadn't been as impenetrable as he had initially thought.
Now, his old enemy was back.

Vladimir acknowledged this fact with a frown, especially as he realised that there was only one vital and essential solution.
Mortimer had to be stopped, once and for all.

Pushing open the doors, Vladimir entered a beautifully decorated and intricate room, filled with light. Immediately, he was overcome by a sense of safety. In this room, not even Mortimer could penetrate these walls with his darkness. Then, positioning himself at the head of the high-table, the centrepiece of such a magnificent space, he acknowledged all those who had gathered with a polite nod of his head.

Subsequently, he spoke.

"My dear friends and colleagues." Vladimir began, smiling at each person in turn. "I thank you all, from the bottom of my heart, for turning up to this important meeting. I also sincerely apologise to those who may have had other plans for this evening." As he spoke, Vladimir's voice had a calm, gentle quality about it but underneath, a strong steeliness could be heard. "Nevertheless, I've called this conference as a result of an extremely serious and critical matter."

For a moment, Vladimir paused to collect his swirling thoughts, before he continued with eyes that were misty with concern.

"Some of you," he continued, "may have felt the darkening change already. Others may not. However, one fact remains clear. Our old enemy, Felonious Magnus Mortimer, has returned."

At hearing this solemn news, a collective gasp filled the room and all shivered, evidently rattled. Each face paled as white as the moon and some even clutched their hearts, for fear of a cardiac arrest. The mutterings abruptly stopped as soon as one of the twelve dared to oppose such an announcement.

"Are you absolutely sure of this news?" The rasping voice of the objector hung like a dark cloud and a deathly silence fell about the chamber. All looked at the person who had spoken in shock. The only person who didn't look surprised was Vladimir, who merely appeared thoughtful. The protester, who looked far younger than he really was, despite his matted, short hair and sharp, inquisitive eyes, continued.

"After all, it's common knowledge that you were responsible for encasing Mortimer in layers of powerful protection all those years ago. Apart from you," he continued, "there's no one else alive capable enough to release Mortimer once more. The general population of our kind just do not possess such incredible powers!"

At hearing such an outburst, Vladimir raised an eyebrow archly. After a momentary pause, he smiled at the protestor for their high praises, with regards to his talents, before sympathy flashed across his aged features. Out of everyone here, he knew that Professor Xandar was the most likely person to object to his announcement. After all, it was in his nature, as the academy's Science teacher, to firmly believe in fact rather than reading the senses, in spite of his own unbelievable abilities. Even so, surely the cold drop in temperature was a sign that he was telling the truth?

Vladimir related this understanding to his defiant co-worker. Even then, as he argued his point, Professor Xandar, or more informally known as Edmond, still appeared to disbelieve him, despite his reasoning.

"Nonetheless," Edmund continued boldly, after Vladimir had finished. "Regardless of your argument, you haven't explained how Mortimer managed to escape the barriers you placed around his tomb, all that time ago? Therefore, Mortimer can't be alive. He just can't."

Now, although Vladimir was an understanding man, considering his associate's background, Edmund was beginning to try his patience. Deep down, beneath that thick skin, Vladimir knew that his colleague's argument was founded on fear.

"But Edmund." Vladimir answered back, his voice superbly calm, although it had a hint of bite to it. "That's where you're wrong, my old colleague."

Vladimir turned to his right and gestured to an extremely beautiful woman, who had long, snow-white coloured hair and an extremely pale complexion, sitting next to him.

"Hecate, will you kindly do me the honour of explaining to Edmund and all those here, who also doubt me, why I am telling the truth?"

When Vladimir had finished, Hecate simply nodded, ignoring those who had shuffled in their seats uncomfortably. Then, she looked at Edmund, directly in the eye, with her piercing gaze.

"Edmund, do you know what special power I was blessed with when I turned sixteen?" Hecate's voice, although soft, was frosty and everyone in the room, apart from Vladimir, twitched in uneasiness. Eventually, after swallowing a number of times, Edmund nodded.

"Of course." He replied slowly, his voice now quiet and hoarse. "Everyone knows that you can communicate with the dead."

After Edmund had finished, the room was so silent that you could have heard a pin drop and all shivered from an unfelt breeze. Gradually, as the silence lengthened, Hecate smiled, her full lips peeled back to reveal perfect, white teeth, which mirrored the colour of her hair.

The tension increased once again.

"Then, surely you can understand the reasons behind Mortimer's escape?" Hecate persisted, her eyes now glowing with an unnatural quality. "The dead spoke to me before Vladimir arranged this meeting. They told me about Mortimer and his dark deals with the otherside – deals that were put in place long before his downfall and deals that have ensured his return."

Once again, the room descended into uneasy friction, as no one dared to speak. All let this statement steadily and painfully digest. After another long silence, bit by bit, realisation dawned upon Edmund. He became even paler than Hecate herself which was, in itself, a fantastic achievement.

"Impossible." Edmund eventually croaked, meeting all with a terrified gaze. "I won't believe what you are both implying. I can't believe it!"

Awakening

Before Hecate could answer, Vladimir cut across her.

"You MUST believe it." He interrupted, his eyes burning. "Unfortunately," he finalised, "regardless of my powers and attempts to prevent such a return from occurring, Mortimer really is back thanks to his connections with evil and so it brings us back around in a vicious circle. What to do about this problem?"

When Vladimir had finished, he looked hopefully into all the faces around him. Much to his sadness, no one appeared to have a solution. Instead, they all shuffled back into their seats, as if trying to seek comfort from the thin leather.

With a disappointed sigh, Vladimir spoke.

"It saddens me to think that not one of you is able to think of a solution to this dilemma." He exclaimed, his eyes becoming momentarily glassy. "Nevertheless," he added, the sadness in his gaze immediately replaced with a profound burning fire. "Despite your silence, I've been able to put an effective plan into action. By tripling the number of 'awakening' scouts presently placed in the field, I believe that we may be able to find our answer, whatever or whoever it entails."

As soon as Vladimir had finished talking, a hushed silence fell about the room. One by one, each person became lost in thought at hearing such a decision. Eventually, someone dared to break the silence with a strangled cry.

"We're doomed!" Professor Xander's words rang about the chamber. He still refused to believe the truth and clearly had very little faith in Vladimir's strategy. So, by the looks of it, did many others, for they began to mutter and whisper to one another, unable to keep the panic and fear out of their voices.

That knowledge wounded Vladimir badly, although refused to show it.

With a stern glare that shut his colleagues up indefinitely, especially Edmond, Vladimir spoke his mind.

"SILENCE!" His cry had the desired effect, booming around the chamber for, as soon as it had left his lips, all fell back into their seats, ashamed of their behaviour - all apart from Hecate, who had simply sat in her chair the whole time, lost in her own darkened world and trance.

Vladimir rose to his feet, hands shaking.

"Yes." He continued, his voice now harsh. "I agree with you all. This is a terrible problem but," he stopped fleetingly, fixing everyone with a blazing gaze. "We're not doomed. In light of the revelations about my plans, like Hecate and myself, we should be optimistic about the whole situation. Otherwise, there really will be no hope for anyone."

When Vladimir had finished, his words hung in the air until Hecate spoke, as she came back from a faraway land.

"What will you do when you've found the solution to this problem?" She eventually asked, her eyes sparkling once more with an unnatural, icy fire.

Vladimir didn't answer at first, himself now the one lost in thought. Ultimately, he turned and fixed her with a fierce stare.

"This academy will offer rigorous training and then, once I feel completely secure with the decisions made, I'll permit the strongest to stand up to Mortimer and his followers."

For the final time, a silence fell about the room, as all considered this proposition. At long last, Hecate nodded in understanding and approval of Vladimir's plan. Soon, this acceptance was followed by everyone in the room, including Edmund.

As everyone began to leave the safety of the meeting chamber and entered the gloomy corridors once more, after Vladimir had declared the meeting closed, no one, not even Hecate, heard his silent prayer.

Whoever hears this, let me be right in my beliefs with regards to this ominous matter. Otherwise, if I'm wrong, then our future will forever be filled with darkness, devastation and death. Subsequently, after he had finished, Vladimir too left the protection of his meeting chamber, before he was swiftly swallowed up by darkness.

CHAPTER 1: ALEX

As far as I could remember, birthdays had always been filled with love, happiness and joy. They were a time when the whole family would gather in either gigantic or tiny congregations to celebrate the anniversary of a loved one's birth. They were a time to rejoice in the notion that a person had grown one year older (if they wanted to be reminded that is). Finally, birthdays were a time of laughter, when presents would be shared, songs sung and past memories revisited. Therefore, on my sixteenth birthday, I woke up early and raced downstairs in the hope of being greeted with the traditional song of 'Happy Birthday.'

As I entered the kitchen, all that I was met with was darkened rooms and freezing cold floors. No family! I was taken aback at first but then, thinking about it, I decided that they had probably forgotten to set their usual alarm. I decided to wait. I waited...and waited...and waited until, an hour later, a dark thought dawned upon me.

My family had completely forgotten that it was my birthday.

Holding back my tears, for part of me still thought such ideas were foolish, I got washed and dressed, doing my best to keep my emotions together. As I made my way downstairs, to the smell of toast and eggs, a small spark of hope deep inside my heart was ignited. Surely, if my parents and older brother were awake now, that would mean that they would have remembered such an important date and, as soon as they saw me, congratulate me on living another year?

As I cautiously made my way into the kitchen, I was welcomed with the usual response.

"Morning Alex." My mother's voice sounded exhausted. "Good night?"

Awakening

"Mmmm." I mumbled, frowning as I sat down to breakfast, watching my mother yawn and stretch. I threw my older brother Matthew, who sat opposite me and my father, who sat next to me, a hopeful glance but both, ignored me.

Matthew was too preoccupied in gazing into space and my father was too absorbed in reading his newspaper.

I will not cry. I told myself as I picked at my piece of toast, barely eating anything. *It's only my sixteenth birthday. I will not cry.*

"What do you have as lessons today?" My mother asked me, plonking her behind onto the seat facing me, before taking sips of her tea and looking over the rim of her cup with expectant eyes.

I will not cry.

"Science first thing." I replied, remarkably managing to keep my voice level. "Then, English and Music."

Suddenly, the sound of the school bus hooting made my mother and I jump. Leaping to my feet, before either Matthew, my father or my mother could say anything else, I grabbed my school bag and raced out the door.

How could they have forgotten the importance of today's date? My brain screamed at me as, with shaking fingers, I climbed the stairs to the bus, before making my way to the back, out of sight. *My birthday, like the norm, happens on the same date every year. Therefore,* the confused part of my brain argued. *How could they have all simply forgotten this fact and acted so "normal" when I entered the kitchen this morning?*

They may have been abducted by aliens in the night? This was a voice from the incomprehensible area of my mind. *Consequently, their behaviour would make complete sense then. Alternatively, they could've simply gone to bed last night fine and then awoken the next morning with amnesia? Sometimes, these things happen unexpectedly.*

"God spare me." I whispered to myself, losing the will to live as more voices of the same illogical nature swamped me with their numerous, absurd theories.

As a result of this mental torture, I found myself dwelling on what had just transpired for much of the depressing journey. Soon, a familiar, comforting voice floated down the aisle, doing its best to relieve me of my torment.

I realised whose house we had just stopped outside of.

"Morning birthday girl."

Well. I thought with some reassurance. *At least David remembered that it's my birthday today.*

Hastily flicking my long, brown hair out of my face, I met his dazzling smile with a small grin of my own, as he plonked his lanky behind down next to me.

"Is everything alright?" He asked, reading my emotions perfectly.

I tried to nod in response to his question, for I didn't want to pass any of my confused state onto him. Soon though, I was shaking my head from side-to-side, desperately trying not to draw attention to myself.

"Not really." I replied, my throat rough. "My family's completely forgotten that it's my birthday."

At hearing this revelation, David looked genuinely surprised.

"What?" He said, frowning. "You're kidding...right?"

I shook my head.

"No." I answered back, feeling my frustration intensify. "When I came down to breakfast, everyone acted as if it was another boring day in the life of the Ravens."

David was clearly shaken by this disclosure. It was written there, on his face. With a small encouraging smile, he threw his arm around my shoulder and tried to see the best in this dismal situation.

Awakening

"Well...perhaps it's your brother's idea of a terrible joke?" He answered, before pulling out a perfectly wrapped present. "And," he added, "when you get home tonight, perhaps your family will throw you a surprise birthday party?" He smiled positively at me although, deep down, I was tempted to remind him that these suggestions were hypothetical. A small part of me saw sense in his reasoning. I wouldn't put it past my brother to do such a thing. My puzzlement lessened. "Having said that though," he added, his emerald eyes now gleaming in excitement. "I haven't forgotten that it's your birthday so go on," he continued, gesturing at the green paper. "Open it up."

David, I thought, *like always, was brilliant at healing a troubled state of mind, not forgetting finding a solution to any troublesome situation.* Consequently, I thanked him silently and concentrated on the gift he had given me.

Slowly, carefully peeling back the green paper, two tickets fell onto my lap. After studying them closely, I let out a squeal of joy when I realised what they were for, causing those around us to stare at me even more strangely than normal. Eventually, when I had collected myself, I threw my arms around David, causing him to blush.

"Oh David, thank you so much." I gushed, overwhelmed. "I've been dying to see 'The Phantom of the Opera' for ages and now I can."

"I know." He grinned, clearly elated with my brighter nature, for his green eyes sparkled in delight. "You've told me that on a number of occasions."

Playfully, I punched his arm, before I realised something.

"You bought two tickets though." I said, suddenly confused. "Who else is going to go with me to see the musical because none of my family will? It's not their thing."

At hearing my puzzlement, David became self-conscious. His cheeks coloured and this reaction seemed to heighten the prominent scar on his face, which ran from the corner of his right eye to the lower part of his chin. David ran his fingers through his wild, ginger hair nervously before replying.
"Well...the decision's completely up to you, but I was wondering if...if...I could take you?" The way he flushed after he had spoken made me smile.
I flashed him a beaming grin.
"You know what, I'd love you to take me," I laughed, carefully packing the tickets away and I was pleased to see David's face glow at hearing this news. "But I didn't think opera was your bag?"
David laughed loudly, breathing out a sigh of relief.
"You have a valid point." He replied, grinning. "Although you never know, I may have a secret passion for that style of music you never knew about."
I raised my eyebrows archly.
"Really." I replied, chuckling. "Well...I'll be very impressed if that's true."
Before he could respond, we arrived at the school gates.
My face immediately darkened.
David sensed the abrupt change in my demeanour.
"What's the matter?" He asked, his green eyes becoming worried, as he watched me hysterically scan the area for some unknown source.
After a few moments, as people around us began filing off the bus, I turned to face him.
"Nothing." I hastily replied, picking up my bag and hurling it over my shoulder. I refused to meet his gaze.
David didn't believe me.
"You're lying." He said, reading the tension in my frame and, once we were off the bus, he pulled me back by my bag.

I shook my head.

"No, I'm not." I forced a smile. "Everything's fine...seriously."

Even then, despite my best convincing efforts, David frowned.

"I know when you're not telling me the truth." He retorted, reading me and my awkward movements like a book. "And now's one of those times." Suddenly, a dark thought came to him. "You're not afraid of someone are you?" He unexpectedly asked, scanning our fellow students' faces. "Because if you are, then I'll go over and sort them out for you!"

At hearing David's correct guess, I abruptly sighed, annoyed. Clearly, David was very good at reading minds amongst his many other talents.

"Look David, everything's fine...really." I smiled at him. The smile didn't quite reach my eyes. "I'll catch you at break...OK?" I added.

He still looked unhappy.

Just before he was about to retort, the bell went, causing his attention to waver. By the time he had looked back at the place I had been standing, I was now half way to registration and praying that, when I eventually went to my first class, the reason for my skittishness wasn't waiting for me there when I arrived.

CHAPTER 2: ALEX

When I opened the classroom door, the 'tangoed' face of Jessica Wademen greeted me.

Ah hell!

"Well, well, well. Look what the cat finally decided to drag in?" Jessica sneered unpleasantly, eyeing up my old skirt, where some of the seams had come undone and my blazer, which had collected an assortment of holes over time.

All heads turned in my direction.

I blushed.

Clearly, I hadn't been praying hard enough.

"I'm surprised she even has the gall to show her face today wearing that!" Jessica continued, pointing at my slowly crumbling school uniform with a horrified expression on her face. "I mean, surely if her father works as a top bank manager, he should be able to provide a decent income for the family, which could be spent on clothes?" She leered at me, laughing spitefully. "But then, silly me, I forgot that he hasn't provided for the family for ages since he was made redundant. These are such sad times."

At hearing this comment, all her girlfriends roared with laughter (who were also as equally orange and plastered in make-up) as well as a group of boys, who had gathered around Jessica and were practically salivating over her painfully low-cut top. I tripped over my shoes in embarrassment, anger rising within the pit of my stomach at Jessica's cutting remarks and her friends' amusement, which caused even more raucous laughter.

Boy did she fit the definition of a 'cow'.

Earlier on in the month, my father had received an unexpected letter from the bank he worked at saying that his: "input was no longer required". This news had naturally come as a shock to the whole family and, whilst we had all pulled together to support each other, particularly my father, in reality, our support did nothing to take away the impending knowledge that our income was due to suffer.

After finally accepting the matter, until my father was able to find another career, my mother had adopted other jobs on top of her previous profession, which had proved to just about ensure our survival. The money she made went on necessary resources and no extras (this list included new clothes). However, due to the fact that we lived in a small town, this news had travelled fast. Although most people did their best to offer support, individuals like Jessica Wademen relished in our unfortunate circumstances.

Just before she could say anything else unpleasant, my Science teacher hurried into the room, in a bustle of irritation and frustration. Instantly, the laughter stopped and people rushed to their correct places. There were some teachers, you learnt, that you should never cross and Mr Nash was one of them.

Clenching my fists, I took my place at the back of the classroom, away from everyone so I could hide my blistering face and allow my inward anger to deflate. I did my best to focus on him instead of the orange form that sat to my near left.

"Good morning class." Mr Nash rasped as he tried to catch his breath. I noticed how his thin, grey hair was matted with sweat and his beady, black eyes began to dart around each face. A resounding monotonous: "Good morning Mr Nash" met his initial comment. Satisfied with this response and the fact that he had stopped wheezing, Mr Nash continued.

"Now…today's task involves the interesting dissection of an Apodemus Sylvaticus, or otherwise more commonly known as a wood mouse –"

Before Mr Nash could carry on, he was immediately cut off by an extremely loud groan delivered by Martin, one of the boys nearest to me.

A vain in Mr Nash's temple throbbed.

"Is there something the matter Mr Crane?" Mr Nash asked Martin, who had suddenly gone incredibly pale.

"N...no sir." Martin stammered, which was met with muffled sniggers from the rest of the class, as he swallowed rapidly, trying to focus.

As a result of this unsatisfying answer, Mr Nash narrowed his eyebrows.

"I should hope not!" He then snapped before he continued with his speech, now moving his glower onto the remainder of the class. "As I was saying, before I was rudely interrupted (he glared once again at Martin) we're going to dissect wood mice in today's lesson. Then," he continued, "after you've finished, I expect you to write down all the different parts of their anatomy and make sure that you do it neatly."

After delivering this emphasised comment, Mr Nash paused once again to glare this time at Thomas who was known, amongst all the teachers, for his appallingly, illegible handwriting. Thomas swallowed, blushing in embarrassment. Subsequently, contented that he had succeeded in intimidating as many students as possible, Mr Nash finalised his speech.

"And so, with that final word of warning, all of you hop to it. You know where the equipment is and, when everyone's ready and I'm happy for you to begin, I'll start handing out the dead mice."

After he had finished, everyone burst into life. All the pupils in my Science class dashed over to the equipment trolley, to select the best utensils as quickly as possible. Soon, the area was filled with people pushing and shoving. Naturally, as a result of this frantic

Awakening

battle, like always, I was the last person to be at the front. When I eventually got to the trolley, I was met with a dismal sight. Every single piece of equipment I needed, of those that were left, was ruined in some way or another.

Slowly, blushing red, I raised my hand.
"What is it Miss Raven?" Mr Nash sighed, his moustache bristling.
"I...I can't use any of the equipment sir." I stuttered, ignoring the heated glances thrown at me. "What's left is damaged or broken."

At hearing this news, Mr Nash tensed.
"Who's responsible for this?" He barked, making everyone jump.
No one spoke.

After a lengthy silence, he continued.
"Well...in that case, all of you will be held accountable and will have a detention after school. What's more," he added angrily. "I've got you again for Science tomorrow. Consequently, when you arrive, I want each of you to give me five pounds to go towards buying new resources and, as there are thirty of you, I think a hundred and fifty pounds will do nicely. For now though Miss Raven," he finished, fixing his furious gaze on me. "I suggest you go to the store cupboard and collect what you need."

Gradually, I nodded, before I slipped out of class. Then, I made my way back to the classroom, hands full. When I arrived, everyone was working in silence. Quietly, I made my way to my work area, desperately avoiding the livid glares I was thrown, particularly from Jessica Wademen. Once I had sorted out my section of the table, I began making a start on dissecting the wood mouse before me. My stomach heaved as I saw its small form and, after I rolled the mouse over, its tiny, glassy eye stared lifelessly back at me, making me shiver in unease. As I cleaned my scalpel, ready for use, my hands began to shake. I brushed them against its soft fur. I couldn't do this.

I just couldn't do this. Thankfully, I was saved by Martin. Jane, the girl working next to him, called out to Mr Nash.

"Sir!" She shouted across the room, her small eyes wide and filled with concern. "Sir. Martin's fainted."

Mr Nash had already sprung up from his chair, after hearing such a colossal thud and was making his way towards Martin's motionless frame before she had finished speaking.

"Thank you, Miss May, but I can see that for myself." He snapped before, when he reached Martin, he tested his pulse. Realising that he would survive, he put one arm around Martin and heaved him to his feet. "Now, when I come back, I want this class to be as silent as it was before Mr Crane graced us with his dramatic display. If not, then there'll be a double detention." Then, practically dragging Martin's limp frame through the classroom and over to the door, Mr Nash headed for the school's medical room.

As soon as he had left, the class erupted.

"Did you see Martin's face when he cut into that mouse and the blood spurted out?" A boy with a freckled face laughed to his friend, imitating Martin's horrified reaction. "What an idiot."

"Yeah." His mate with a dopey expression answered. "Yeah. It was well funny."

I was the only one, out of the whole class, who continued to contemplate cutting the mouse. Jessica saw this and decided to draw attention to my actions.

"Look." Jessica rapidly screeched, pointing at me with her perfect, pink talon. "The teacher's pet's afraid of getting into trouble!"

Once more, I blushed red as the whole class burst into laughter.

"What's more," Jessica continued, her lip curling. "She's responsible for getting us all into trouble and having to fork out money that'll be wasted on more boring equipment, as well as having a detention tonight, meaning that I'll miss my appointment with the tanning salon." Her eyes narrowed. "So," she added maliciously, smirking. "With that being said, who's with me for teaching her a lesson that she'll never forget?"

Jessica's eyes glinted wickedly, as a resounded "yes" from the rest of the class filled the room. As a result of this cold treatment, I shook with anger at the fact that everyone in my class was willing to pin all the blame on me, even though I had done nothing wrong.
It was so unfair.

Suddenly, I realised that Jessica was holding the scalpel that she had used to dissect her mouse. Its blood dripped all over the floor.
My anger abruptly turned into fear.
Surely, she wasn't going to use that on me? My brain screamed. *Surely someone is going to come to my rescue when they realised her twisted intentions?*

I shot a frightened glance at random faces in the room but they were too focused on me, in their own anger, to notice the scalpel looming ever closer.
Jessica noted my mounting terror.
"Scared, are we?" She muttered, so only I could hear, playing with the scalpel that she had now slipped under her sleeve, although not completely out of my sight. "Well...you should be."
Jeese, I thought, fear choking me. *I was being targeted by a 'tangoed' psychopath!*

As Jessica walked ever closer, I left my work area and started to back up, until I felt the wall of the classroom behind me. It was then that I knew I couldn't escape. Immediately, the world started swimming before my eyes. My breathing increased and I started to hyperventilate. I couldn't breathe.
I just...couldn't...breathe.

As I almost lost consciousness, it happened. My whole body began shaking uncontrollably, as an indescribable feeling of complete power raced through me. It was at this moment that the fire sprinklers in the room burst into life and screams of people being soaked to the skin filled my ears in a cacophony of noise. Everyone began frantically clawing at their ruined hair and make-up. To my relief, I saw Jessica drop the scalpel in her surprise.

As the water poured down around me, I was the only one who stood there unmoving, after the shaking had stopped, eyes glowing with an abnormal light. The water from the sprinklers mixed with the blood on the tables and floor. Then, I was consumed with the overwhelming sensation that I could do anything I wanted and no one, not even Jessica Wademen, could stop me.

I rounded on Jessica.

"That's it." I snarled and she cowered when she saw my unnatural features, along with everyone else who had stopped screaming and were now focusing their terrified attention on me. "I've had enough of your torments. For far too long, you've bullied me and made my school life a misery. Now," I smiled coldly and all shivered. "I shall have justice."

After I had finished, I raised both my hands up before me in an involuntary response. Then, the water around us slowly began to bend and move until it had formed a huge, liquid vortex. As soon as people saw this, they began to scream in terror and tried to escape. Some even dove under the tables. There was nowhere to run. The doors were locked.

Somehow, I had made sure of that.

Once the vortex had been created, I commanded it to swallow Jessica. As soon as the thought had entered my brain, Jessica didn't even have time to scream before she was entombed in the swirling, liquid whirlpool, coughing and spluttering. It was as this event occurred and I saw Jessica's petrified expression that the whole world seemed to freeze. Time stood still.

Awakening

Slowly, I grinned. Finally, I had the power to destroy everyone who had done me wrong over the years. Finally, I had the power to wreak revenge on all those who had laughed at me and did nothing to stop Jessica's cruel taunts. Finally, I was the victor and not the victim. Just as I was going to deliver the last blow, my morals returned.

Stop. They screamed at me. *Stop. This is wrong.*

But it feels so good. I argued back. *Now, I have the ability to crush my enemies, like they've crushed me.*

But you're not a murderer. They disagreed. *Yes...those before and all around you have done you severe wrong in the past. However, if you go through with your intensions, you won't be able to survive with the guilt. That, my friend, is a fact.*

Gradually, my heart was filled with understanding and fear. I heeded these words of wisdom. Jessica fell to the ground in a sobbing, spluttering and sodden mess. Immediately, all crowded around her, to see if she was alright. It was only after she had confirmed that she was fine, or as fine as she could be after nearly drowning, that the entire class, including Jessica, looked frantically in the direction I had previously been standing.

Much to their shock and relief, I was gone.

CHAPTER 3: ALEX

As I tore through the school building, past the gates and out into freedom, one thought consumed my mind.
What the HELL had just happened?
One minute my life had been completely "normal" in as much as I went to school, knowing that Jessica Wademen was waiting for me and was about to extend my unhappiness further, despite the fact that it was my birthday, when BOOM. Something deep inside me had 'awoken' and it had been wonderful.
No. I thought. *Not wonderful.*
Instead, it had been weird, freakish and damn right terrifying and had resulted in me almost killing someone. Then, whilst their life had hung in the balance, I had contemplated about killing even more people. How could I suddenly go from a person who had struggled to dissect an already dead mouse, to someone who was willing to murder a human being? There was no logic to it. Also, there was no logic to what occurred when I'd actually commanded that water to surround Jessica. It simply defied belief, science and understanding.
As I raced towards the park, I knew I hadn't dreamt the whole thing up. I could feel, actually feel this new source of energy seeping out of every pore in my body. For the first time in my life, feeling the wind race through my hair, I felt alive and it was wonderful. I slowed down when I saw the enormous willow tree in the near distance, which overlooked the local lake, sighing in relief. I was tantalisingly close to my favourite destination for contemplation, space and reflections. When I reached the bench situated underneath the tree, I sat down, groaning as my brain desperately tried to absorb all this fresh information.
This is just unbelievable. I thought, now turning my hands over in wonder. I remembered how they were responsible for shaping and

Awakening

taming the water from the sprinklers and tracing the lines on them with my finger. *It's all just too good to be true.*

As I mulled over this new-found knowledge, a dark thought came to me. If this really hadn't been real and instead, it had been from the creative section of my brain, I could prove it right here, right now, in front of me. Scanning the area to see if anyone was watching and seeing no one there, I extended my hands out before me. Then, closing my eyes, I imagined the water swirling, bending and twisting until it formed the clear, vivid image laid out in my mind.

When I opened them, my heart stopped.
"Yep, this isn't a dream, a hallucination, a delusion or anything of that nature. Your ability to create a dolphin, out of the lake water before us, is proof of that fact, once and for all."
A man's voice suddenly sounded behind me.

As soon as this had occurred, I nearly jumped out of my skin, spinning around to face him. As I did so, the liquid dolphin collapsed and the water fell back into the lake, for he had broken my concentration. Immediately, I scanned my eyes up and down the stranger's body, taking him in with interest. The stranger was undeniably handsome and he had short, brown hair and brilliant, blue eyes. He was also dressed in casual clothes which, although were lose fitting, betrayed a hint of a toned physique underneath.

As he approached me, I registered his dazzling smile, which was one of those that had the ability to make anyone automatically grin back, no matter how hard you tried not to or how emotional you felt. However, whilst he walked closer, much to my disappointment, I realised that he was in his late-twenties. My smile dropped. I guess that the goddess Venus wasn't on my side with this fine specimen of the male gender.

As he came to a halt, the stranger beamed at me, as if he had just found a long-desired prize.

My stomach resumed its fluttering.

"Alexandra Raven, I presume?" He abruptly asked in a rich, deep voice and holding out his hand, displaying long, rough fingers. "It's a pleasure to meet you."

At first, my brain seemed to shut down, as my senses were overloaded by a flood of emotions. Once I had noted what he had said, I ignored his gesture, despite the fact that he was gorgeous, before leaping sharply to my feet. Although he was undeniably handsome, at the end of the day he was still some random stranger, who had suddenly appeared out of nowhere, wanted to talk to me and who knew my name. The term 'Stranger Danger' flashed before my eyes. Therefore, no matter how hot he was, I wasn't going to let my guard down...yet.

Make a run for it! A voice in my head commanded me. *Make a run for it, before it's too late.*

This voice was clearly sensible. However, sometimes I wasn't sensible, especially when intrigue was involved.

Despite my pounding heart, I heard my cautious reply.

"W...who are you?" I asked him, suspicious. "And how do you know who I am?"

The stranger must had seen the mistrustful gleam in my eyes because he set about correcting the situation, returning his hand to his coat pocket. He looked at me in interest, his blue eyes glinting.

"Please forgive me for disturbing you? I mean no harm." He answered, smiling warmly.

Bizarrely, from his tone and features, I relaxed a little.

Damn him and all his sexiness.

Awakening

"My name is Jack Carter and I'm one of the many scouts who has been sent by the incredible Vladimir Alcaeus to seek out new teenagers, such as yourself Miss Raven, who've just 'awoken'."

When he had finished, Jack saw the stunned look that past over my features. I tried so hard to digest all this information. Jack also noticed my subsequent expression and must have heard the screams of 'Psycho Alert', alarm bells and all, that reverberated around my brain. His face changed instantly. Even so, his face expressed an emotion I was least expecting. Rather surprisingly, his reaction was to chuckle.

"Look." He said kindly, gesturing to the bench beside us. "Sit down. Clearly, I've got a lot of explaining to do."

For a moment, I paused, unsure of how to proceed. There was still time to make a quick get-away. After a few seconds, I nodded, complying too his offer. This was mainly because I was suddenly overcome with dizziness, as a result of the jumble of emotions and thoughts that were causing throughout my body.

I collapsed onto the bench in a heap.

That's the natural response of someone who's just 'awoken'. Jack's voice sounded in my head and I jumped, my mind becoming instantly clear and eyes wild.

"Y...you spoke in my mind." I stammered, frantically trying to register this fact and looking at him in blind panic.

Despite my shaken reaction, Jack merely smiled.

"That's my talent, along with reading people's thoughts." He answered normally, gazing at me and smiling kindly. "Much like elemental control is yours."

I threw him a surprised but puzzled look and my heart started doing a million beats per second.

"W...what?" I answered back, still battling an internal war, after listening to what he was saying.

Jack simply grinned.

"Surely you must know about elemental control?" He asked me.

I shook my head, trying to regain control over my body. Deep down, I had an idea, but my stomach seemed to have consumed all the butterflies on the planet. I also wasn't sure I wanted to hear my suspicions confirmed.

Jack sighed, mystified by this fact, before trying to relieve me of my confusion.

"Well...there're five elements in total." Jack began. "These include: earth, water, fire, air and spirit. Normally, people are able to control one of these elements. No one knows of anyone who can control all five. By the looks of it though," he concluded, "you can control the element of water."

At hearing this news, my mouth moved up and down like a guppy but no sound came out. Somehow, this all made perfect sense and yet, why was a small part of me still holding back?

"But...but that's i...impossible!" I stammered, trying frantically to absorb this brain overloading information. "What you say is insane."

Jack chuckled at my incredulous expression.

"I know." He replied, grinning. "I had the same reaction when my scout broke the news to me about this amazing change. However," he added, "you have to know that what I say is true." Jack smiled at me warmly before continuing. "'Awakenings' are to do with some form of mutation, which happens to the cells in our body, at a certain stage in our lives. Still," he added, seeing that I was struggling to come to terms with this life-changing event. "Forget about that as all you need to know is that, from this moment onwards, you've been blessed with an incredible gift. Few people ever get the chance to experience what's just happened to you, for it's a rare occurrence indeed. Therefore," he finalised, "my advice is to accept the fact that

Awakening

you've 'awoken', because you can't reverse the change and embrace your new powers."

After he had finished, I looked at him bewildered and mystified. This was just so crazy and absurd that it was painfully hard to believe. I sighed, trying frantically to find a rational explanation for what had happened and what was happening to me at that particular moment in time, as a light, electrical current whizzed around my body.
I failed miserably.
"But why have I only just developed my so called "powers" now?" I cried, having not quite finished denying this life-changing circumstance. "Surely, it would make more sense if my "powers" 'awakened' right after being born? Then, this information wouldn't be such a shock to the system."

Jack answered this for me in a split second.
"You've only just developed your powers now because your powers only ever 'awaken' on your sixteenth birthday." Jack replied. "I don't know why it happens like that but, thinking about it logically, as a child, you would cause more havoc if your powers 'awakened' then than if they 'awakened' now. I suppose that's because if you were younger, a.k.a. a baby," he added, "you'd have no understanding of the enormity of this situation. What's more," he continued, "what would your parents say and do when they realised that their beloved baby was "abnormal"?" (It was Jack's turn to air quote). "Some may go to the police. Some may seek medical help and some." Jack's face turned dark. "Some, may lock their child away or even…"

Jack trailed off, looking at me in a haunted way. I got the idea, feeling a lump form in my throat and shivered in unease. A silence fell between us momentarily, before Jack continued.
"At least now you can reason and explain to them not to be afraid or better still, they may already know what's happened to you. These

powers tend to run from generation to generation, although the 'awakening' gene may not be active in such families for decades. Luckily, I was one of those few who inherited an active 'awakening' gene, as my mother likes to remind me from time-to-time."

When he had finished, I sat there in stunned silence. Then, fear, panic and alarm took control over all the logical thoughts that tried to invade my brain. Deep down, I knew that Jack was telling the truth. What other reason could explain the incredible events that had just occurred and how I was feeling? And yet, frustrating as it might sound, I just couldn't accept this explanation.

Don't fight it. I heard Jack say in my head and I snapped my neck up, fixing him with a terrified stare. *As hard as it is, it does get better.* Jack's eyes burned into mine. *I promise.*

It was then, as I sat gazing into his face and saw the powerful emotions gathering in his startling, deep blue eyes, that somehow, in spite of my brain screaming at me that Jack was clearly a lunatic, I accepted his mind-blowing explanation. Sighing for the hundredth time, I spoke, rubbing my eyes, for I suddenly felt exhausted.

"T...this really is r...real then?" I eventually stated, my voice cracking slightly. "It's really happening to me and not all part of my imagination." I didn't need to look at Jack as I spoke.

I already knew what his response would be.

"Yes." Jack responded. "It's real. It's as real as you and me."

Suddenly, the image of Jessica struggling to breathe, in the middle of that watery vortex I had created earlier, popped into my mind. I let out a small sob of overwhelmed realisation. God, I had almost killed Jessica. I could be a murderer right now.

But you're not! Jack's voice sounded sharply in my head.

Slowly, dragging my aching heart off the ground, I met his stern gaze.

Awakening

I saw what you did earlier. He continued, his gaze unwavering. *And when I saw the potential of your talent, as that horrid girl struggled to hold onto life, I was afraid that you really were going to kill her. All the same*, he added, making sure that our connection wasn't lost. *You have to know that when our powers initially 'awaken', they're usually entirely unpredictable and feed off the first emotions they can find. Consequently, when your powers 'awoke', they fed off your fear and rage and then directed it onto all the people who had, and were, tormenting you at the time. That's why you acted in the way you did.*

Jack's eyes were alight with a fierce fire as he talked. I could see his passion burning within their depths. However, he was not finished and his final words ensured that all the dark thoughts that clouded my mind and heart were swept away.

Finally, what I'm about to say comes from more than just me being a scout. It comes from the heart as I'll tell you now, in all the years I've been doing this job, I've never seen such control as you have over your powers already. Therefore, I'm deadly serious when I say that I know you'll go on to do great things and that you should keep your head held high, because you've a bright future ahead of you Miss Raven.

When Jack really was finished, I let all my emotions go. It felt right and Jack took me in his arms. Eventually, I stood looking at him, eyes shining with acceptance. For the first time in my life, I felt as if I had found a place where I could belong, despite the fact that it had taken sixteen years to reveal itself.

"So..." I eventually asked, now somewhat intrigued. "What's next?"

Jack smiled at my curiosity.

"Well." He replied, grinning as he watched me sponge away the last of my tear streaks with the sleeve of my disintegrating blazer. "Vladimir Alcaeus welcomes you to join his leading academy for people like us. Then, once you're there, you can learn how to control your powers, until you're ready to return to living amongst the human race and carry on with your existence, if that's what you desire. If not," he added, "you can live amongst our kind, like I do. However," he finished, "I warn you that even then, although you can still use your powers, you must keep them a secret, in order to protect our existence."

As he spoke, I listened to all of this in silence, until the time came for contemplation.
"If I go with you, will I have to leave my family and friends?" I finally asked.

Jack thought for a moment, considering my question, before nodding.
"Yes. Until you're stable enough and can control your powers well, you'll have to live at the academy. Then, once we deem you read, you will be allowed to see them again."
Gosh. I thought. *This is so hard. I loved my parents and brother to bits. Also, all of us were under so much stress, due to my father's unfortunate circumstances. Therefore, could I really leave them for this?*

David's face floated before my eyes. I let out a small cry of realisation. I would never be able to see him again, until I could control my powers that is and that could take goodness knows how many years. Besides, what about the show that he was going to take me to for my birthday?
You won't be able to go. Jack said in my mind, throwing me a sad smile. *It would be too dangerous for those around you.*
But he means so much to me. I thought back. *I've known him ever since we were five. We've practically grown up together.*

Jack nodded sadly.
I understand, he answered, *but we can't put innocent lives at risk. Also, how would you feel if something went wrong and David...*

Awakening

Jack trailed off, leaving me time to fill in the blank space.
I knew he was speaking the truth.

At the end of the day, I would never forgive myself if something happened to David. That was too awful to comprehend. Deep down, this knowledge did nothing to take away the pain that I felt.
My heart caved.

Drawing back from my deepest thoughts, I vowed silently that, if I ever saw him again, before I left to go to the academy, I would tell David what had happened to me, regardless of the rules and regulations I was due to commit myself to. I owed him that much.
Then, mentally, I accepted Jack's offer.
You've done the right thing. He replied, taking my hand. *Both your parents, brother and David will be proud of you and I'm sure that they'll understand.*

I smiled at his response, before another thought unexpectedly came to me out of the blue. It was a dark thought and my heart rate quickened once more. Jack must have noticed my stiffened reaction. As soon as he scanned my current thoughts and locked gazes with me, he spoke, relieving me of my troubles.
"Don't panic. We have it all under control." He checked his watch before continuing, smiling. "My guess is that by now, our specialist team have made sure that all those who witnessed your 'awakening' have had their memories modified, that you have been announced "ill" and have therefore had to go home."
I looked at Jack amazed.
"Wow." My voice was breathy and my mouth slightly agape. I swallowed a little before speaking again. "So...you're telling me that you have the resources to actually erase people's memories?"

Jack flashed me a grin.
"Yep." He said, smiling. "Our team is very specialist, although "erased" sounds far too harsh for my liking. It's more modified."

39

I chuckled before I realised that I was now surprisingly fired up and excited.

"So...what do I have to do to finalise all of this?" I asked, adrenaline pumping around my body.

In response to my question, Jack pulled something out of an invisible pocket. As he did so, I noticed for the first time that he had some form of a marking in the middle of his right hand, which was in the shape of a circle. Directly in the middle of this circle, there was an image of a brain, which was black in colour.

Before I could question him, Jack abruptly thrust a small, metal circular object into my right hand. As soon as it touched my skin, I felt tremendous pain, as it burned into my flesh, scarring me forever. I let out a cry of shock and agony, as steam began to rise up from underneath the metal. However, Jack held on tightly to my wrist and hand in a vice-like grip, preventing me from moving. Eventually, as unexpectedly as it came, the burning vanished and the metal circle dropped to the floor, making a clanging sound as it hit the cold earth, sending up a small amount of sizzling smoke.

Wrenching my hand from Jack's, I lifted it to my face to inspect the damage. The mark was still smoking and a nasty-looking, red rim had formed around the edge of the circle. As I lightly touched it with my other forefinger, I jumped at its sensitivity.
Bloody hell that stung.

Whilst I inspected it closely, there, in the centre of my hand, was an image of a single wave, blue in colour and slightly raised and red.
I threw Jack a cold and furious look.
"What the hell is this for?" I shouted, waving my hand and the mark, in Jack's face. "You've literally branded me."

Jack looked embarrassed, as he picked up the metal circle.
He pocketed it before replying.

Awakening

"I know and I'm sorry but it's just something we all have to do when our powers 'awaken'," He answered and showed me his own mark, which I had seen earlier. "Look, this is my mark. The brain, in the middle, tells others of our kind, for it's invisible to humans, that I'm a mind-reader, like the wave on your mark tells people that you can control the element of water. Also," he added, "the marking system allows us to travel from one place to another and ensures that the council are able to keep track of everyone's movements, in case something bad happens if we lose control. Then, once they've assessed the situation, they can take the necessary action."

Slowly, I let this information wash over me before I sighed. "Surely the council can think of a less painful way of travelling, communication and criminal control?" I asked him, when the mark had cooled down and no longer throbbed.

Jack chuckled at this remark, but shook his head. "Unfortunately, many people, including myself, have had the same thought. However, according to the council, for the sake of a few minutes of pain, that mark on your right hand will be permanent. Really, it's the best solution."

As I contemplated his justifications, I wiggled my fingers and winced as the mark stung. Most of the pain and redness, much to my surprise, had rapidly gone in a matter of seconds. Nevertheless, it was still sore.

Oh, why couldn't the mark have simply appeared on my hand, like in those normal, magic movies? I thought angrily, as I clenched and unclenched my fist. *That would've made my life so much simpler and pain free.*

Remember that this is your life we're talking about here, was the answering thought. *That says all you need to know.*

"Now," said Jack suddenly, making me jump. "I feel that it's time to break this news to your family. Then," he added, smiling at me. "At precisely seven o'clock tomorrow morning and not a second sooner, I'll come to collect you, before taking you to the academy. That being said," he continued, with an amused grin. "Although I wish you well in celebrating this event, I also advise you to pack as soon as possible because trust me, I don't want to be hanging about waiting for you to find your underwear."

At this last comment I laughed, although slowly, my features darkened. If my family had forgotten to celebrate my birthday, then they were highly unlikely to rejoice in the fact that I had just 'awoken' which meant that, for the past sixteen years of my life, my powers had lay hidden and dormant, out of sight. These views were founded on the fear that they had no idea that the 'awakening' gene even existed. After all, not everyone may be aware of their family history, despite how remarkable the whole thing was. Instead, their likely reaction would be, if I told them, to go deathly pale and then cry or instead, go insanely beetroot red and demand that I should be taken to the hospital to have my brain scanned for a possible, clinical disorder.

As a result of these fears, I told myself that I would not say anything until the right moment came. Nodding to myself in satisfaction, I turned to meet Jack's gaze once more. He smiled at me knowingly. I shivered.

I'm sure everything will be explained when you get home. He said mentally, eyes sparkling.

"What's that supposed to mean?" I answered back, but he refused to elaborate. I sighed. "Look. Unless they already know about my powers," I added, "I'm not telling them anything for their own protection. All I'll say is that I've been offered a place at a highly prestigious academy, due to my exceptional ability at manipulating science.

Jack laughed but still didn't say anything until we were standing outside my house.

"I'm sure that they'll understand." He answered. "However, for now, remember - 7 o'clock on the dot."

"I know." I replied but, as I went to thank him, silence greeted my ears.

Frowning, I turned around and shivered.

Jack was gone.

Shuddering, I was unnerved by his unexpected disappearing act, although I supposed that Jack swiftly vanishing into thin air was something I could live with after all the freakish things I had seen, done and heard so far today. Even so, what I couldn't live with was the terrifying knowledge that, after telling my family what had happened to me, if I ever did, they would disown me or worst still, cut me off from all life and existence.

CHAPTER 4: ALEX

When I entered the house, the absence of life, particularly after being with Jack so long, took the meaning of 'gloom' to a whole new level. I knew that my mother and brother were still at work and my father was probably at the local job seekers centre, due to the fact that it was coming up to lunchtime. All the same, knowing that I had to spend the rest of the day, my birthday, with all these experiences and thoughts zooming around my mind and not able to tell anyone any of it if I wanted to was tough.

Throwing my bag down into the hallway, I made my way into the lounge. The cries of "HAPPY BIRTHDAY ALEX!" nearly deafened me as I rounded the corner. As I stood there like a rabbit in headlights, painfully slowly, I registered the ecstatic faces of my mother, father, granddad, grandma, uncle and auntie all beaming at me in joy. Then, I took in the gigantic birthday banner, with my name behind them hanging over the back wall, as well as the congratulations banner hanging in the side dining room. Finally, I registered the balloons, party hats and best of all, the food on the table, topped with a homemade, chocolate birthday cake made traditionally by my grandma.

My heart and mind went into overdrive.

As I gazed into every face, I became overwhelmed, especially as I was astounded that they had gone to such great lengths to make this day special. The whole show, including food, must have cost a considerable amount of money and, in view of our present, rocky circumstances, I felt the luckiest girl in the world. That being said, rather embarrassingly, my emotions got the better of me. My mind was also reeling from my recent discoveries, making me an emotional wreak. Therefore, after I had undertaken a final sweep of the room, my response to everything was to lose it.

"What the hell is all of this?" I snapped, feeling the negative emotions I had held pent up inside me hit me all at once like a steamroller.

At seeing me anger, my mother rushed over, paling and throwing her arms comfortingly around me.
"Oh Alex, honey, why are you so mad?" She asked, looking worried.
I threw her a 'seriously?' look.
"I'm mad," I retorted, "because all morning you've made me feel like you'd forgotten that it was my birthday today."

As I raged, a part of me felt silly and very, very ungrateful, considering everything that my family had done. The rest of my family stood there looking awkward. When I had finished, my mother paled even more, before shooting a troubled glance at my father. After reading her face, he slowly took a step forward, his blue eyes apologetic.
He placed a hand on my shoulder.
"Both your mother and I are very sorry for putting you through what we did earlier." He answered and I read the sincerity in his gaze. "After you raced out this morning, clearly upset, we realised that what we had done had been wrong but we had reasons behind it."
I stiffened.
"Reasons like what?" I retorted.
My father sighed.
"Well...we...we weren't sure if you...if you'd..." He trailed off, looking back at my mother for support.
She shot him an encouraging glance before he continued.
"Well...w...we...weren't sure if you'd 'awoken' because if you had, we...we were going to have a double celebration."
I felt deflated, like a popped balloon.
"W...what?" I said, overcome with shock, as I registered this comment.

Seeing my changed state, my father bent down to my level.

"We know all about Vladimir's special academy." He finally said, his eyes now swimming with remembrance at a past event when his new wife, then nine months pregnant with their first child, had told him all about her ancestors and the fact that any of his children could have 'superpowers' as she had called them. This news had been an extreme shock to the system although, eventually, he had come to terms with the crazy matter, after many sleepless nights and cans of beer. "And we know that the academy was created for extremely gifted teenagers and I don't mean gifted in the usual sense."

When he saw my overwhelmed reaction, he smiled before gesturing to the whole family, who were all nodding in agreement.

"We know that you've 'awoken'. We received confirmation earlier from Vladimir himself." My father smiled. "Therefore, it would be wonderful if you could show us your new powers. I know everyone's desperate to see what you can do."

After my father had finished, I gazed at each excited face and I felt my anger leave me. Yes. I had been hurt by the fact that I had genuinely thought that my family had forgotten that it was my birthday. However, as I saw my family's reaction, utter relief flooded through my veins. I realised that no member of my family was going to lynch me or take me to a mental hospital to be probed and prodded. I blushed, feeling very silly and brattish indeed. Boy had I learnt my lesson. I should never have doubted the intentions of my family. They knew best in this instance, just as they had always done.

As a result of this situation, I met this relief and overwhelming realisation with a small smile and I hoped my next action would wipe the slate clean. I thought about making the water in the glass on the table move and briefly swirl about the room, before returning to its original location.

Awakening

On command, it did just what I wanted.

When I was finished, my work was met with applause and gasps of surprise and delight.

"Oh darling, that was amazing." My mother cried, before planting a kiss on my cheek. "And your father and I are truly sorry for this morning."

I returned her kiss, smiling.

"I know." I replied, squeezing her hand. "I'm sorry for getting so worked up about the whole thing and for what I said earlier." Then, after kissing my father lightly on the cheek, I repeated this ritual with everyone who had gathered to celebrate this occasion.

It was only as people began to help themselves to food, after a resounding song of "Happy Birthday" echoed repeatedly off the walls, that I realised I had a number of questions I desperately wanted answers for. I went over to my mother, who was finalising last minute food in the kitchen.

"Thank you for what you've done." I said, smiling. "Really, I wouldn't have minded just watching a movie at home with you, especially as money's so tight right now, although I'm curious, how were you able to organise this celebration if you were supposed to be at work?"

As soon as I had finished talking, after putting down a tray of sausages and mini cheeses, she gestured for me to sit on a kitchen chair (ironically the same chair that I had sat in earlier when I thought they had forgotten it was my birthday).

Then, she spoke.

"I worked my magic and managed to have the day off." She answered. "However, it does mean that I'll have to work an extra day next week but what the hell, my daughter comes first." She flashed me a grin and I returned her smile with a small one of my own.

When she was done, I relayed the next question - why my brother wasn't here to celebrate the good news.
This time, she looked at me sad and strained.
"Your brother?" she echoed in a small voice and her eyes became glassy. "He...well...let's just say he and I had a disagreement earlier, which means that he's not going to come to your party, although he better be back this evening or serious words will be had."
Sensing that she wasn't telling me the whole truth, I pushed further.
"It's about me isn't it?" I asked her, reading her reaction perfectly. "It's about me and my new powers?"
After I had finished, she let out a small gasp, looking at me strangely before she bit her lip, an internal battle raging inside her.
After a few moments, she relented.
"Yes Alex," she sighed. "It's about you and your powers. You see, when I told him the good news, regarding your 'awakening', he took the information hard and was reminded of his own birthday and the fact that he hadn't been blessed with such a precious gift —"
"How did you know about 'awakenings' and about the academy?" I blurted out, interrupting her, as I couldn't contain my turmoil of emotions any longer. "I remember father saying earlier that it was common knowledge but, at the time, I got distracted so now I want answers. Why didn't you tell me all of this before today?"
My mother sighed wearily at my outburst.
"I knew you'd ask these questions one day." She answered, trying to smile at me and rubbing her temple with her fingers. Eventually, when she continued, her eyes had a faraway look about them. "We knew about the possibility of receiving powers on your birthday because the 'awakening' gene has been passed down in our family, from generation to generation," she began, echoing Jack's earlier explanation. "Your ancestors, who've in the past been blessed with

Awakening

such a gift, have all come from my side of the family. Therefore, when I reached sixteen, my parents, like your father and I did for you and your brother, waited to see if I 'awakened'. Unfortunately," she continued, "it was not to be. Consequently, they didn't inform me of the situation until a long time afterwards."

She threw me a small, troubled smile.

"It's always been thought best not to tell your child this kind of information before their sixteenth birthday in case they didn't 'awaken'." She added. "For some teenagers, the knowledge that they were unable to have incredible powers has proved to be too much for them to bear. For that reason," she concluded, "we didn't tell you because we wanted to protect you, just like we protected your brother who thankfully, didn't do anything stupid when we informed him about the matter years later." She paused for a moment, dwelling on past history.

I suddenly felt awkward. I felt as if my powers, instead of being a blessing, were now a curse as, understandably, I felt isolated in the knowledge that my mother, in addition to my brother, were always going to feel that inkling of: 'why not me?'. My brother's refusal to attend the celebrations was proof of that notion and it hurt so much, in particular the remembrance of how close we had been. Now, thanks to my newly acquired talents, our relationship could forever be shrouded in shadow.

My mother brought me back from my troubled thoughts.

"Still...our prayers were finally answered when you, after countless years of waiting, were the next kin to have such a wonder bestowed upon you." She gave me a soft smile. "And when we received confirmation from Vladimir himself." Her eyes were full of wonder. "Your father and I are so proud."

I felt my heart heave. Even so, there was one query left I wanted to clarify.

"You would've told me about everything eventually?" I asked hopefully and my mother nodded.

"Of course." She clarified. "After all, one day, you may have children of your own who may also 'awaken' as, although it's an extremely rare occurrence, it's not impossible."

Slowly, I felt the wounds my heart had taken heal, although that dark cloud of discomfiture still hung over us.

"Thank you." I said finally. "I respect your explanation and, in the circumstances, I believe that you did the right thing."

She gave me a weak smile.

"I'm glad you think so kiddo, although I assure you, it wasn't easy."

I nodded, reading the truth in her eyes before she brushed the topic away, now excited with the prospect of me leaving to start my new life.

"So...when do you leave?" She asked eagerly.

"Tomorrow." I replied, trying to smile but, even still, this did nothing to take away the awkwardness I felt. "One of Vladimir's scouts came to tell me the good news today, after my powers had 'awoken'. He's coming to pick me up at seven o'clock tomorrow morning."

My mother's eyes beamed with pride at this news.

"Oh Alex, honey, I'm so excited for you." She cried. However, her eyes darkened at a saddening realisation. "Although I understand that you may not see us for a long time, until you can control your powers?"

I nodded in conformation of this fact.

"I'm going to miss everyone so much." I cried and she threw her arms around me, stroking my hair.

"Oh darling." She replied. "We're all going to miss you too, but you can e-mail us, can't you?" She asked hopefully, before drying her eyes and mine to the best of her ability. "After all, your father and I are still dinosaurs in terms of social media."

Awakening

I nodded.

"Yes." I answered. "I'll e-mail you and father as many times as I can." She smiled at this news, before ushering me out of my seat.

"Now." She said, taking my hand and leading me back into the lounge. "I want you to have fun tonight. At the end of the day, this should be a night to remember – for the right reasons."

Slowly, I nodded in understanding.

One final question popped into my mind.

"So...who was the last person in the family to have powers?" I asked my mother, intrigued, which caused my sadness to momentarily disappear.

My mother smiled knowingly, pleased to see that I was no longer gloomy.

"The last person in the family to have powers was your great grandfather – Alistair Silverstone." She said grinning. Clearly, I realised, our family liked the names beginning with the letter 'A'. "He was very talented, although his power was much more of a shock to the system than yours, believe me, in particular when his parents, or I should say mother, Maria, found out."

"Why?" I asked, now very intrigued.

My mother chuckled.

"Well...let's just say that when Maria came home and saw Alistair having a full-blown conversation with 'Old Bessie' the cow, she thought her son had somehow been involved in a serious accident since she'd last seen him. Nevertheless," she added, "it was only after her husband had told her about the 'awakening' gene, numerous glasses of alcohol and many an argument, that she finally decided to accept the truth."

I really laughed at this explanation and so did my mother.

"So...he was a real Doctor Doolittle?" I asked when I had managed to control my laughter.

My mother nodded, smiling.

"Yes." She replied, laughing. "Yes. I suppose he was. After Alistair left the academy, he became one of the best veterinarians and animal right campaigners in the world. Having said that though," she added, a sparkle appearing in her eyes. "Although many were desperate to know the secret behind his success, when his family and he eventually died, they took his secret to the grave. After all, you're supposed to keep your powers hidden from the outside world, aren't you?"

It was my turn to nod. However, her last comment roused my initial sadness.

Although I tried to join in the festivities to the best of my ability, when the rest of my family had left to go home and I made my way upstairs to pack my case, my heart was heavy. On the one hand, I couldn't wait to begin my new adventure. In spite of everything, before today, I had thought only awesome superheroes like 'Spiderman' and 'Superman' were fortune enough to have powers. On the other hand, I was dreading leaving my family and, of course, David, who I still hadn't seen since this morning. I was also worried my brother would never want to talk to me again.

CHAPTER 5: ALEX

I woke up to the sound of someone gently tapping on my bedroom door. Groaning, I realised that I must have fallen asleep halfway through packing. Snatching a look at my alarm clock, I hurriedly started throwing the remainder of what I needed into my suitcase, before answering the door.

"Come in?" I called out, my back to the door.

When I turned around, expecting to see my parents or hopefully my brother, I was both surprised and relieved.

"David!" I cried, dropping the pair of pink knickers in my hand on the floor and throwing my arms around him, making him blush the same colour as the pants. "You don't know how much it means to me to see you."

David threw me a pleased look, although his face became stricken with concern, once the pink tinge had somewhat faded.

"The same can be said for me, although no offense Alex, but you look awful."

"Thanks." I retorted laughing but, glancing at the mirror in front of me, from the redness of my eyes, I realised that I couldn't disagree. "Tell me about it." I abruptly muttered, walking over to the mirror and gazing at my drained features, tracing the outline of my tired eyes with my fingers. "I feel awful."

Sensing him place his hand supportively on my shoulder, I spun around - only to find myself inches from David's face. As soon as this had happened, I felt my heart rate increase, much to my surprise and, to make matters worse, I blushed. Due to the unfamiliar responses my body was undergoing, I quickly widened the gap between us.

David didn't say anything.

"I missed you so much at school today." He eventually whispered and I desperately tried to lose the awkward heat in my cheeks. "When I heard that you'd left Science, because you were ill and had to go home, I was beside myself with worry, particularly after seeing you badly on edge this morning. What's more," he added, "I failed my Maths test."

I groaned.

Thankfully, my earlier embarrassment had subsided.

"Was it the same test that I'd helped you revise for every single day?"

He nodded.

"Yep. It was that same wonderful test that both of us found utterly riveting to discuss."

A silence fell between us before I replied.

"Sorry." I finally mumbled.

David chuckled.

"What are you saying sorry for?" He retorted. "It's only a test. I'd rather fail a thousand Maths tests than hear that you were lying, in hospital, in a critical condition. Trust me when I say that, after hearing gossipy horror stories all day, I'm extremely glad that those stories are not true."

I felt my heart heave at his words, before I realised the time had come to break both the good and bad news I had pent up inside of me. Taking his hand in mine, I led him over to my bed, sitting down on the edge, to which he followed suit. All the humour vanished from his face the moment he registered the tension in my frame.

"David." I said slowly, avoiding his piercing gaze. "There's something I have to tell you."

At seeing my nervousness and, at hearing the serious tone in my voice, David threw me a worried and pained expression.

Awakening

"Please tell me that you haven't killed anyone?" He blurted out, with what looked like fear and horror in his eyes.

As soon as David had made this shocking exclamation, I couldn't help but choke. This was because I was one of the last people on Earth who would have ever thought of committing such a crime. Clearly, even though David knew this, logic and sense had apparently abandoned him.

You nearly did earlier though. This traitorous thought popped into my mind. *And the worst part, you were actually enjoying it.*

No sooner had the inner voice spoken, I slammed my defences down.

I refused to acknowledge the truth in these words.

"No." I said, shaking my head in disbelief. "No. I'm most definitely have not killed anyone. However, what I'm about to say is seriously life-changing."

Slowly, I took a deep breath, before I told him what had really happened that morning. I didn't care that I was technically, potentially breaking the rules.

David was my *best friend*!

"I didn't leave school earlier because I was 'ill'." I explained, my voice shaking. "I left school because something both incredible and insane happened in my Science class."

This time, I looked into his confused gaze.

"I have powers David." I blurted out and, once I had started talking, I couldn't stop, even though David looked at me as if I was crazy. "I have amazing powers, which 'awoke' today and have been passed down in my family from generation to generation. What's more," I added, "these powers mean that I'm able to control the element of water with just my mind. I mean, it's all just so weird and amazing. Can you believe it?" I laughed nervously. "I still can't."

When I had finished my rambling and saw the sudden frightened look in his eyes, I decided there was nothing else I could do but to prove this fact visually and verify that I wasn't mad. Taking the glass of water from my bedside cabinet and placing it on the floor in-between us, I imagined the water dancing around us, swirling underneath our arms and legs and around our separate bodies, before finally leaping over our heads. The water did just that until, despite his increasingly pale complexion, I really did go crazy.
I tested my abilities.

I made the water transform into different types of animals, including a regal lion pretending to roar, as well as seals being chased by killer whales, which used our bodies as pieces of floating ice to duck and dive under. Then, I created different forms of transport, such as an aeroplane, which zoomed over our heads, before landing on a pretend runway, as well as a cruise ship, carrying thousands on an imaginary journey. Finally, I finished with a raven, crying out to its mate, before the two of them flew off into a pretend sunset.

When they had disappeared, I allowed the water to fall once more into the glass. Then, I braced myself for the hardest part — David's reaction. As I met his gaze, my heart fell. His eyes were filled with so many emotions that I simply lost count. Wonder and awe were mixed with terror and shock. Eventually, David stood up, turning his back on me as he shook, his breathing ragged.
He broke our connection.

Much to my agony, the silence between us lengthened, until I could take it no longer.
"David?" I asked, standing up and going to place my hand on his shoulder. "David. Say something?"

As soon as my skin made contact with his shirt, David stiffened, as if he couldn't bear my touch. I felt my heart snap. He took a step

Awakening

forward, causing my hand to slip from his shoulder. Sighing, he turned to meeting my heartbroken eyes with his unreadable ones and ran his hands despairingly through his hair.

"Alex..." his voice was croaky and painfully dry. He tried to cough, licking his lips but even then, he just didn't know what to say. Ultimately, he sighed. "Alex...I...em...I'd better go."

At hearing his words, my heart, which had already suffered a tremendous blow, was further ripped into even more pieces. I realised that my worst fears were rapidly becoming true.

I tried so hard not to cry.

"No!" I whimpered, barring the door with my body, as he made a grab for the handle. "No. You can't go yet. You haven't been here that long and there's food still left over from my birthday, if you're hungry? I even think my Mum's made some awesome non-alcoholic cocktails if you'd like to try one, o...or perhaps we could watch the complete collection of 'Star Wars' movies? I know my mum wouldn't mind you staying over tonight."

My mind was on overload as I rambled on, frantically thinking of any excuse, which would keep him there. As I saw the internal battle David was fighting and the sadness and troubled sentiments in his eyes, I stopped talking, stepping aside to let him pass, which he did. He barely glanced at me.

David was halfway down the stairs when I called down to him, trying to keep my voice steady as I played, what I hoped would be, my trump card.

"I'm leaving tomorrow to start school at a special academy." I told him. He didn't even turn around. "That means that I won't be at school anymore and possibly, when I eventually graduate, I may never come back."

Although David had carried on walking as I first spoke, I saw him falter at my last words. My emotional blackmail had seemed to work. His shoulders tensed, as well as his hands, which clenched as if he was fighting something.

Please turn around? I prayed silently. *Please, please turn around?*

Sadly, my prayers weren't answered. Breathing heavily, he walked outside the house, shutting the door behind him with a little more force than was necessary, not once looking back.

Damn you! I mentally screamed, finally allowing myself to give into my emotions. *You've stuck with me and comforted me through thick and thin and now, when I need you the most, you turn your back on me and leave. Furthermore, I may never see you again.*

Jeese! A second, rational voice entered the internal conversation. *Ease up on him a bit. The poor guy has just witnessed something that completely defies logic and belief. That something has come from the girl he has known ever since he was five. Therefore, give him time to mull over and consolidate what he has just seen. Then, when it has sunk in, he may come back to you.*

Don't make me laugh. I retorted angrily. *Did you even see the look of horror on his face as I transformed the water? Never in my life, since I first met him, has he ever looked at me like that. For that reason, there'll be a fat chance that he will ever come back to me. We're better off without each other.*

"Alex." My mother's voice called from the kitchen, shattering my mental argument. "Is it my eyes or has David just left? He wasn't even here five minutes."

I tried to keep myself together as I replied.

"Yeah." I said, my lip trembling. "Yeah. David only popped in to see if I was alright and had to leave because of homework."

I hoped it was a good enough excuse, even though I heard my mother go to reply. I couldn't cope with being on the stairs for much longer. With tears streaming down my face, I ran into my bedroom, slamming my door sharply behind me, causing the ornaments in my room to rattle and slid down the wood the other side. Then, burying my head in my hands, I sobbed.

CHAPTER 6: ALEX

The shrill sound of my alarm clock woke me up at exactly 6:30am. Sighing, rubbing my puffy eyes and then stretching, I rolled over and heaved myself out of bed. The next half an hour went by in a blur. Before long, I stood outside with my old, shabby-looking case by my side, waiting for Jack to make an appearance.

I had already said goodbye to my parents yesterday night, after pulling myself together as much as I could about David, who had left a gaping hole in my heart. I checked my phone for the millionth time. Not one message from him. I tried so hard not to cry.

As I stood there moping, I realised that the one person I hadn't said goodbye to was my brother, who I assumed hadn't returned home until very early this morning, given away by the snores coming from his bedroom. This knowledge hurt, especially as we had always been so close, although I was relieved to hear that he was OK. Nevertheless, this did nothing to take away from the pain in my heart. I may never see him again and, if I did, it could be a number of years down the line. Yet, even then, he may not want to see me.

At seven o'clock exactly, I checked my watch, before looking around me. There was absolutely no sign of Jack.
"Glad to see you're raring to go." Jack's voice suddenly sounded from behind me. I let out a shriek as I spun around, heart hammering, before I glared up into his beaming face. "It makes a change to see that someone's taken my warning about being ready on time seriously. That way, you don't have to face the consequences."
"You nearly gave me a heart attack!" I scolded him, clutching my chest with my free hand once I had got my voice back. "You shouldn't sneak up on people like that. I didn't even hear you arrive."

Jack flashed me a grin.

"That's because I've mastered the art of vanishing and reappearing unexpectedly." He said, winking at me and waggling his fingers, before his face turned serious. "However," he concluded, "we can't afford to stand here talking. We need to go like now. I have a schedule to keep to you know. Are you ready?"

Sighing, I nodded.

"Good." He replied, before he took my marked hand in his. Thankfully, my mark no longer stung, although I did notice that, rather shockingly, it was now glowing a vibrant blue colour. It's was beautiful. This changed through the moment our marks touched. They instantly glowed a bright white, causing me to gasp. "Then let's go and make sure," he added, "whatever you do, don't...let...go."

I didn't have time to collect my thoughts.

Immediately, the pavement beneath us fell away. I let out a shriek whilst we dropped through the ground, as if we had just taken a plunge on the tallest rollercoaster, minus the straps. Far below us, I saw a gigantic, black vortex swirling hungrily. I screamed at this sight, filled with utter terror as very gradually, Jack and I were pulled towards its darkening core. I felt the urge to do the one thing Jack warned me not to in my panic.

I loosened my grip.

"NO!" Jack shouted, over the tremendous noise, his eyes filled with panic at my response. "NO. DON'T...LET...GO!"

As soon as the words had left his lips, I felt his hand tighten in mine. There was no way I could escape now. It was a good job he held me tighter for, abruptly afterwards, the vortex seemed to inhale an almighty breath. The two of us span faster and faster in such a way that I was almost violently sick. Then I, screaming all the way and keeping my eyes firmly shut, whilst desperately trying to manage my heaving stomach, along with Jack, was swallowed up by complete blackness.

CHAPTER 7: ALEX

When I eventually opened my eyes, Jack and I were no longer in an ear-splitting vortex. Instead, we were standing in a gigantic, grassy field. From the smell of salty air, I guessed that we were somewhere near the coast.

"What...what the HELL just happened?" I asked Jack, staggering with dizziness and paling as I desperately tried to tame my stomach in the hope that it would not bring up the piece of buttered toast I had eaten for breakfast.

Jack laughed, looking dashingly handsome as usual and absolutely fine. He stretched with ease, much to my envy and watched me struggle to regain control of my balance and organs with an amused look on his face.

"Well...let's just say that you've had your first taste of how we move from one place to another, unless you're already blessed with the skill of teleportation. If it's any comfort," he added, "the experience gets better each time."

I groaned at his explanation, clutching my throbbing head.

"Surely the council can think up a better way of transportation than being dragged into a gigantic, black vortex and then feeling worse than ever before, once you have arrived at your destination?" I answered back after gulping lungsful of fresh air. "So far, in my opinion, they're doing a pretty shocking job!"

Jack chuckled at my annoyance.

"Well...that's been another question regularly proposed to the council but the answer is always the same – what's the point in changing our habits when that particular method of travelling gets you from A to B with hardly any damage?"

I threw Jack an "are you serious?" look.

"Hardly any damage!" I retorted, clutching my groaning stomach. "You call this hardly any damage?"

Jack laughed before I sighed, once more consumed with irritation.

"Well...if that's how the so called "council" views it, then they well and truly suck. Why can't they make the vortex rainbow coloured and noiseless instead of looking and sounding like a deafening, gaping void that's going to rip you into a million pieces?"

I was going to continue venting out my anger and sickness on Jack when, after looking down at my feet, I groaned in further annoyance. My trainers were completely covered in mud. Clearly, it had rained here, wherever here was and, what's more, it had rained a lot.

My day just kept on getting better and better.

"Why didn't you tell me to wear wellies instead of these?" I scowled at Jack, as he practically had to heave me out of the smelly, sinking mud-hole we had landed in. "My trainers are ruined."

Jack threw me an apologetic glance, as he saw the error of his ways, which had not only caused me grief, but had ruined his smart black shoes as well.

"Well...I would've told you if I'd known that this was where we would end up." He answered, grimacing as his own feet started to sink. "Clearly, they decided to change meeting locations since I last saw them and forgot to brief me."

I sighed at hearing this news, even more ill-tempered.

"Typical." I retorted, sulking. "So damn typical!" However, when I saw a girl who looked around my age suddenly fly over my head and into the distance, closely followed by her scout, I forgot my exasperation. "Wow." I abruptly gasped, watching her fantastic display. "This really is happening isn't it?"

When Jack saw what I was looking at he grinned.

"Sure is." He replied, smiling. Nevertheless, when he saw how far I had sunk, he turned his attention back onto me. "However, if we don't get a move on, nothing else will happen because we'll be spending the rest of our days trapped in a muddy bog."

I noticed what he was talking about and, groaning in disgust, heaved myself through the sludge.

"Why couldn't I have her talent?" I sighed as the mud now clung to my legs and ran into my shoes. I watched the flying girl land gracefully outside what I presumed was the gigantic, gothic-looking academy. The tassels on her beautiful, figure-hugging dress fluttered in the breeze, as her shoes made contact with the ground, although I was surprised she was wearing a dress in this weather. (Thankfully, the dress was so figure-hugging that it had preserved her modesty). I also decided that she was immune to the cold, unlike I was, which was rather surprising, considering the usual British weather and season. "It would not only save me time but money as well."

Jack frowned at my comment. Clearly, he was the kind of person who always tried to see the best in situations, no matter how bleak or exasperating they were.

"Don't think like that." He replied, helping me over a particularly horrible patch. "Your talent is just as good as hers." Nevertheless, when Jack tripped and fell head first into a puddle of brown sludge, spitting out grass and mud and cursing until he was blue in the face, he rapidly changed his tune. "On second thoughts," he groaned, hastily wiping the grime off his face. "To be able to fly would be extremely handy right now."

CHAPTER 8: ALEX

When the two of us finally reached the academy, after much huffing, cursing and groaning, we both looked like mud monsters. Mercifully, we were greeted by a kind and thoughtful lady, who looked in her early forties, with short brown hair and soft, green eyes.

As we entered the hallway, the girl who could fly was now making her way up the beautifully ornate wooden stairs, carrying her own case, which looked very expensive. She had not long finished saying goodbye to her scout, who had a superior look on her face and she was extremely pretty, with long, blond, curly hair, blue eyes and a well-formed figure. When the girl who could fly met my eyes and saw my dishevelled appearance, she sneered at me in displeasure.

What the hell had I done to deserve such an unpleasant reaction? I thought, my insides prickling. *Clearly, her angelic-like features didn't match her personality.*

In the end, I glared at her, fuming. Seeing my response, she quickly turned around and, as she did so, she did nothing to hide the revolted look on her face, before she carried on towards her destination.

I change my opinion. I mentally said to Jack, who had seen the heated glance between her and me but said nothing. *I'd never trade my powers for someone as obnoxious as her.*

Before he could reply, the woman with the green eyes reached us in a bundle of shock.

"Oh...just look at the pair of you." She cried, frowning. "What on earth possessed you to try and walk through the grounds, let alone in inappropriate footwear? They're literally swimming in mud."

Awakening

Jack sighed at the sound of her words, using the back of his grubby hand to wipe his sweaty forehead which, unfortunately, only resulted in him smearing more mud on his already grime caked face. "There must have been some form of miscommunication." Jack answered grumpily.

That was a serious understatement. I thought and I believed I saw a small smile linger on his lips, as he helped me with my own case, before he continued.

"I wasn't told that you'd moved the meeting point since I last saw you yesterday in London. Consequently, when we arrived, I expected to land on a concrete pavement, not in a boggy field."

At this news, the woman's face flickered in puzzlement. Then, she threw her hands up in the air.

"Well." She said, shaking her head. "I can't get my head around that. As far as I was aware and informed, everyone was told about when and where the meeting point would be." After seeing Jack stiffen at this news, she waved him off with her hand. "There's no use arguing over this matter, as the damage has already been done but," she added, once again seeing Jack's desperation to interrupt. "Please be assured that I'll inform Hannah about the matter as soon as possible. After all, organising and checking travel routes is her speciality."

Noticing my shivering body, she rapidly turned and smiled warmly at me. Out of the corner of my eye, I saw Jack's shoulders relax.

Clearly, she was a woman of her word.

"For now, though, I want both of you to go to our ground floor bathrooms and have a nice, hot shower." She said, leading us along numerous corridors, which were decorated with antique ornaments, flowers and oil paintings of ancient men and women, who frowned down upon us from above. "Then," she continued, "we can sort out introductions and formalities for you my dear (she looked at me) as well as ensure that you (she now looked at Jack) are ready to resume your schedule."

When she had finished, Jack nodded at this remark, his face twitching in annoyance. Clearly, he had an infatuation about being on time. All the same, when we reached the bathrooms, which branched off into separate rooms for men and women, both of us sighed, relieved.

"Now." The kind woman said, helping me place my case just outside the entrance. "When you've both finished making yourselves more presentable and comfortable, you'll find clean towels and clothes waiting for you inside the door. Then," she finalised, "when you're ready, come back along the way you've just walked until you once again reach the main entrance where I'll be waiting for you (again, she looked at me)."

After she had finished, Jack and I then thanked her for her kindness. Once she had bustled off, I said my goodbyes to Jack.

"Thank you for all that you've done." I said blushing, now strangely feeling shy in his presence, as we parted. "Hopefully, we'll see each other again?"

He smiled down at me.

"That's OK." He said, grinning. "It's all part of the job description, although I'll say that it's been a pleasure knowing you and I'm sure we'll meet again. However, for now —"

Au-revoir. Jack spoke the last word in my mind.

I smiled back at him.

Au-revoir. I mentally replied. *Until next time.*

Subsequently, with a last grin, he turned and disappeared into the men's bathroom, leaving trails of mud on the recently polished, wooden floor.

After a few moments of silence, it was my turn to leave. Checking that my case was fine, I made my way into the woman's bathroom.

Without a shadow of a doubt. I thought, as I pushed open the carved, wooden doors. *I was sure as hell looking forward to a lovely, hot, long soak.*

CHAPTER 9: ALEX

As I entered the bathroom, I noticed that there was an ornate, crystallised clock hanging high above my head, fixed to one of the marble walls. It read 8:30am. I couldn't believe an hour and a half had gone by since Jack had picked me up this morning, although I assumed time had raced on because of how long it took to reach our current destination and to wade through the thick, slimy concoction that currently clung to my clothes and bare skin.

Walking around the room, I took in my surroundings. The bathroom was very spacious, with marble floors, walls, sinks, toilets, statues and, may I add, much to my delight and excitement, an enormous bath in the middle of the room. Perfect. The only trouble was that the room didn't take privacy into account.

On the far wall were several mirrors, all of which reflected back my mud-splattered features and clothes. Unfortunately, there was no shower curtain to hide behind as I carefully undressed. As I stripped down until I stood naked in the centre of the room, I prayed that no unsuspecting persons would happen across me, as I enjoyed my solitude. Otherwise, I contemplated and shivered at the unwelcome thought, they were in for a definite shock.

Crouching down near the side of the bath, I turned the water on. Much to my surprise and happiness, in a matter of moments, it was full to the brim with wonderfully, soothing hot, pink liquid, bubbles and foam. Slipping into the water, I let out a moan of pleasure as my body reacted to this amazing liquid.

As it soothed my aching muscles and made my skin silky smooth, the bubble bath seemed to remove all traces of the vile and smelly slime that had initially clung to my skin. There was also shampoo and conditioner, located in a fancy, popup lid connected to the side of the tub which, after sinking down underneath the water

Awakening

and scrubbing my body with the pink soap, I used on my hair until I felt clean once more. Subsequently, as I leaned back, I decided now was the perfect time to try my powers again.

Closing my eyes, I formed an image in my mind, before I lifted up my dripping hands. I heard and felt the pink water around me begin to twist and turn. Eventually, when I opened my eyes, I realised I had been successful in my creation of a pink water fountain, where I was the centre statue.

That was when, from behind me, I heard the scream.

CHAPTER 10: ALEX

Spinning around, I hastily started pulling bubbles and foam to cover my body, as the surrounding water cascaded down all around me, from my broken concentration. The water drenched my already soaking body and created a tidal wave, which covered the whole surface floor of the bathroom.

As I raised my head and met the intruders shocked but awe-stricken face, I was relieved that what water had fallen back into the tub just about covered my modesty. For a moment, both of us said nothing.

Then, we burst out laughing.

The girl standing before me had an adorable laugh, which made her tight, black, long curly hair bounce up and down against her shoulders. As we grinned back at each other, I noticed that she was wearing a loose, baggy t-shirt, faded jeans and flower-patterned wellies (well, lucky for her, she must have received the briefing about the change in meeting locations) and I realised that we had a similar dress sense. Eventually, after laughing so much, she doubled over, wincing as she clutched the stitch that had formed in her side.

Once I had controlled my own laughter, I found the breath to talk again.

"God. You scared the living daylights out of me!" I wheezed, wiping my tearful eyes on the back of my wet hand.

The girl threw me an "are you kidding?" glance - a scarily good impression of my renowned expression, although she was smiling.

"I scared the living daylights out of you?" She retorted, when she had in due course managed to breathe herself. "More like the other way around. I came along to collect you only to find some serious craziness awaiting me in the form of ten-foot-high, pink water, which seemed to have a life of its own."

As she talked, I laughed.

"Sorry about that," I finally replied. "It was all my doing."

She nodded after my comment, although she flashed me a grin.

"I guessed that when I saw you in the middle of the bathtub," she replied, before she added something which totally threw me off guard. "Although may I just say that you've got some awesome skill there for someone who's only just 'awoken'."

I beamed back at her after she had finished.

"Thanks." I answered, although I was puzzled by her last comment. "But how did you know that I've 'awakened'?"

The girl laughed at my perplexed expression.

"Relax." She replied and unconsciously, from the casual tone in her voice, I felt my shoulders fall. "I know about your 'awakening' because I'm also in the same boat." She threw me an excited grin. "And Mrs Sampson told me, when she asked me to collect you earlier."

All of a sudden, she cursed after turning her head to look at the clock now high above her head.

"Oh lord." She exclaimed, hastily wiping up the water-soaked floor with a fluffy towel. "We'd better get going. Everyone's waiting for us, or more you and I bet they're getting touchy. After all, I was supposed to be back in the entrance hall ten minutes ago."

She threw me over gorgeously soft, golden towel and spare clothes. Then, she slipped behind the wall, near the entrance of the bathroom, to give me what little privacy was available, whilst I dried off and changed.

"It didn't help that I got lost on my way here." She added. "This place is massive."

As I pulled on my underwear, I fired questions at her.

"What do you mean 'everyone's waiting for me'?" I asked.

She replied swiftly.

"Well...there's a group of us newbies, including me and you, who arrived at the academy this morning and Mrs Sampson wanted to give us a tour of the academy when we're all together. However," she concluded, "the tour can't officially start until you're ready, hence why we really, really need to get a move on."

I nodded in response to her reply, as I quickly pulled on my t-shirt and a silence fell, before I asked my second question.

"So...what's your name?"

The girl laughed.

"Well now she asks me that question after all this time." She replied before continuing, smiling brightly. "My name's Jasmine, but everyone just calls me Jazz. What about you?"

As soon as she had replied, I was reminded of the Disney princess from the film 'Aladdin'. She even looked like her which was cool.

I answered her question.

"My name's Alexandra, but everyone just calls me Alex."

Jasmine giggled.

"That sounds pretty badass." She said. "Are you badass?"

After she had finished, it was my turn to laugh, as I finished dressing. Jasmine had no idea how ridiculous that sounded, particularly after what I had been through.

"Nope." I replied, before practically stumbling out of the bathroom door in my rush to get to the entrance hall as soon as possible. "I've never been the badass type."

My amusement faded when a horrid realisation suddenly passed over me.

"Where's my case?" I asked her, panicking for I couldn't see it anywhere and racing around the hallway like a madwoman.

It was as if it had vanished into thin air.

Awakening

Much to my exasperation, Jasmine's response was to laugh at me, as I hysterically looked in every nook and cranny. She didn't even offer to help. Eventually, she solved the problem, after drying her teary, grey eyes with a handkerchief.

"Calm down." She retorted, reining me back by my shirt. "And stop panicking. Mrs Sampson sent some of the staff to take your case up to your room earlier. It hasn't been stolen, if that's what you thought?"

After hearing this, I glared at her.

"So...now you decide to tell me, after laughing at my confusion?" I snapped, crossing my arms in irritation.

Sensing that she had aggravated me, she backed off.

"Look." She said, holding her hands up in surrender. "I'm sorry for laughing at you, but the fact that you were trying to look for a huge case inside that tiny flower pot over there just set me off. You couldn't possibly have thought that it was in there?"

I sensibly avoided her accusation. Still, despite her sincere apology, I didn't completely trust her.

"Are you absolutely sure that they took my case up to my room?" I asked her, scrutinising her features.

She laughed even harder than before.

"Have I mistaken this building for some form of interrogation centre?" she asked, smiling.

When she saw my un-amused look, she sighed.

"Look. I promise that your case is fine. I saw them head up to the dormitories with it, if that's any comfort but," she added, seeing the glint of mistrust still lingering in my eyes. "If it helps, I'll cross my heart. Happy now?"

Slowly, I nodded before, hesitating slightly, we started strolling down the corridor. We walked in uneasy silence for most of the time.

I was the one to break the tension.

"Mrs Sampson." I finally asked and I heard her exhale noisily, relieved that I was talking to her again. "Is she the kind lady with the short, brown hair and green eyes?"

Jasmine nodded.

"Yep." She replied. "That's her."

Again, a silence fell but soon, I was the one to speak once more, as I studied the mark in the middle of her left hand in interest. It was an image of a sun, surrounded my two big, fluffy clouds and was gold in colour.

I had no idea what that mark meant.

"So..." I asked her, not sure how to approach the matter but nonetheless intrigued. "What power do you have?"

Jasmine threw me a grin, unconsciously tracing her mark with her other forefinger after I had finished. It briefly flashed a golden colour, before dimming. However, before she could answer, we arrived in the entrance hall and were greeted with one very worried face and several irritated ones.

I blushed.

Mrs Sampson hurried over to us, her face lined with anxiety.

"Thank goodness you're here at last Alexandra. I was getting very worried that something nasty had happened to you in the bathroom. Still, as you're here now, I can finally get on with the introductions."

Clapping her hand on my shoulder, she smiled at me, clearly relieved. Then, she released me, before turning around, until she faced everyone.

All of us looked at her intently and, despite the fact that she had begun her formal opening, I still felt the occasional heated glance. Standing next to Jasmine, I pulled my hair down over my face, so that it covered my burning features. After a few minutes had passed

Awakening

and feeling that most people were no longer looking in my direction, I quickly snuck a look at the others in my group.

My heart fell at one particular sight.

Over the other side of the hallway, was that pretty, unpleasant girl who could fly. Sensing that I was looking at her, she turned around, caught my eyes and threw me a particularly horrid glare, distorting her beauty fleetingly. I went slightly red at this reaction, especially as I couldn't understand her motives. However, ever since overcoming my fear of Jessica Wademen, I found the confidence to glare back at her once more, which she met with bristled dislike, before she turned away from me, scowling.

Smiling to myself, I was just about to turn away when I saw her catch my eye and whisper something nasty to the girl next to her, causing both of them to burst into a fit of giggles. That earn't them a heated glance from Mrs Sampson. Nonetheless, that didn't detain them from their clear amusement, which went on in occasional bursts of sniggers and exchanged, knowing smiles.

Clearly, I thought to myself, when I finally managed to peel my attention away from their hushed mutterings and sidelong glances at me. *I had encountered another Jessica Wademen type, minus the copious amounts of fake tan. Lucky me.*

To distract myself from the unpleasant comments being made, which were obviously directed at me for some reason or other I couldn't comprehend, I concentrated on assessing the others in my group.

In total, there were ten of us, who stood in a semicircle in the middle of the grand hall, facing Mrs Sampson. I guessed that the friend of the girl who could fly, who had raven coloured hair and a permanent snooty look on her face, had some form of power relating to animals, as her eyes were remarkably hawk-like. Then, next to her, was an extremely tall boy, with savagely cropped, brown hair, sun-kissed skin and who was bulky in size. Giving him the once over, I determined his power instantly, in particular from the way he constantly crushed his hands together and clicked his knuckles. Really, it didn't take much thought.

Next to him, there were a pair of twins, a boy and girl, who were both extremely pale and had big, blue eyes. Their most prominent feature was their blond hair, which permanently stood up on end, as if they had just been severely electrocuted. Therefore, I decided, if I was right in my analysis, I would definitely try to avoid them in the future. After all, water and electricity, as a combination, is one best to be avoided. That left Jasmine, two other boys and another girl. Jasmine, I assumed, would tell me of her powers soon. Consequently, I focused my detective skills on the remaining two boys and girl. One boy was practically as thin as a bean pole, with medium length, curly blond hair, a pale complexion, green eyes and a vague, daydreaming expression.

As for the girl, she was Chinese, had long, brown hair pulled back with a headband and a small, petite, slim figure. She was also constantly moving, unable to keep still as she hung onto every word Mrs Sampson was saying, which I was distantly paying attention to. Due to her jittery movements, I guessed that she could have powers related to speed.

The last person in the group held my attention the longest. It was for a reason I couldn't explain. He was of average height and build, although he was slightly broader in his shoulders and wore a thoughtful expression on his face, as he listened to what Mrs Sampson had to say. This boy was exceptionally pale, which only succeeded in heightening his jet, black hair and wore casual clothes, including a scruffy, leather jacket, jeans and shoes. These items of clothing were in complete contrast to the girl who could fly, who practically screamed "designer fanatic" in her expensive dress.

Awakening

As I gazed at him in intrigue and interest, I noticed that his eyes were a deep, rich honey colour, behind his glasses. They seemed to dance with an inner strength that gradually drew me in.
Soon, I lost myself in their glow.

It was as I stood their gazing at this boy, in some form of trance, that he must have sensed my presence. Suddenly, he turned his attention away from Mrs Sampson and met my gaze with a small smile, the golden hue of his eyes lighting up in abrupt awareness.

As our gazes met, I became tomato red, embarrassed to be caught looking at him in such a way. I hurriedly turned my attention back to Mrs Sampson, who was finishing what she was saying. For a moment, I sensed that he was still looking at me, skimming his eyes over my features and sussing me out. Eventually, he politely dropped his gaze and returned it onto Mrs Sampson.

My heart pounded with adrenaline, as I let the heat slowly drain from my burning cheeks.
I decided to nickname him: 'Mystery boy'. Mrs Sampson's abrupt tone brought me back to attention, snapping me out of my emotional reverie.
"So," she said, looking at each of us in turn. "With that being said, let's start the tour. When we've finished, I'll leave you to explore the academy for the remainder of the day. However," she continued, "I ask you to keep your noise level to the minimum so that you do not disturb lessons, which will be continuing to run regardless of those who, like you, have arrived new to the academy. Lastly, at precisely seven o'clock, dinner shall be served in the dining hall and," she added, "a word of advice - make sure that you arrive early, otherwise you may go hungry."

Once she had finished, she immediately began to walk up the gigantic, ornate staircase in order to begin the tour. We were about to follow her when she turned around, for the final time, remembering something important.

"Oh," she said, chuckling to herself. "I almost forgot to remind you that you'll find your timetable waiting for you in your new room, which will start tomorrow (this announcement was met with small groans from some, although they were silenced by Mrs Sampson's sharp glance) and you'll be sharing your room with one other person, which has been randomly allocated. A notice will be sent out later in 'The Grand Western Wing' for you to see with regards to this matter but," she added, sensing our restlessness. "For now, let the tour begin."

And so we were led throughout the grand building, from the dark, dusty basement at the bottom of the academy, to some of the classrooms, where fellow students sat either in sleepy boredom or passionate interest. Eventually, we reached the high attic, at the top of the academy, accessible only by an ancient set of spiralling, wooden stairs, which was a space encouraged by the teachers. Mrs Sampson explained to us that this room was built to allow students to work in silence, away from the bustle of the main building. It also boasted an amazing view of the surrounding woods and the sea in the far distance, which could be seen on clear, sunny days.

As soon as we reached the attic room, I hurriedly raced to the window in the far right-hand corner of the wide space, followed by Jasmine and looked out of it in delight, feeling the cold, fresh air hit my face. Instantly, I knew that this would be one of my favourite places to work. Jasmine gasped at the wonderful views of the surrounding countryside and we grinned at each other, knowing that we clearly shared a deep love of nature.

I jumped as Mrs Sampson's amused voice sounded in my ear.

Awakening

"I can see that you feel at home here already." She said and I turned around, meeting her smiling face with eyes filled with excitement, nodding vigorously.

"Yes." I whispered, still overcome with exhilaration, as I watched fellow students frantically working at the tables, over the other side of the room and on the huge, comfy chairs dotted at random. "This academy is amazing, although I think that this area is my favourite." She chuckled at my contentment, grinning down at me.

"Your clear happiness reminds me so much of myself when I started here many years ago." She replied, laughing. "This place was my favourite space too." Then, still smiling, she finished the tour, stating that it was our time now to explore the academy and its wonders.

As I climbed down from the window, helped by Jasmine, I noticed 'Mystery boy' watching me in deep curiosity, for he had overheard our mini conversation. Once more, I blushed before turning away and, avoiding his piercing gaze, I asked Jasmine if she would like to explore the grounds and the lake with me, before we could find out our new roommates.

Much to my relief, she met this question with a definite nod of enthusiasm and we scanned the room one last time. Subsequently, Jasmine and I headed off down the spiral stairs in the opposite direction to the girl who could fly, her hawk-like friend and the intriguing boy with the golden eyes. Then, we found ourselves outside, in the chilly sunshine and, this time, both of us were wearing appropriate footwear.

CHAPTER 11: ALEX

The grounds themselves were vast. As we explored as much of this area as possible, trying to see through the gathering mist, we walked along many winding, hilly paths, which were accompanied with gigantic, tall hedges either side. Along our journey, we would happen upon small, open spaces where, before us, in stunning glory, were different fountains made of expensive marble. These fountains sprayed jets of water high above our heads in some form of elaborate dance. Furthermore, powerful statues, depicting different kinds of creatures and humans, both mythical and real, chiselled to perfection, pointed us towards our intended destination.

When Jasmine and I came across these areas on our exploration, we giggled in amazement and delight, before sitting down on the fountain edge and resting our tired feet for a moment, hearing the birds call around us and allowing the wind to rustle our hair. Apart from these noises, we couldn't hear anything else. It was then that Jasmine revealed her powers to me. I had put my feet up on the fountain edge and was looking into the murky water, watching the koi carp beneath us swim lazily about, when the mist around us thinned into nothingness.

Suddenly, glorious sunshine fell down upon us like a ray from heaven. The moment this happened, I looked up at Jasmine, startled, as the warmth seeped through my thick coat, heating my cold skin. Seeing the swirling colours in her eyes, I realised that she was responsible for the change in weather.

I laughed in delight and wonder.

"Jazz." I abruptly cried, jumping up and down in excitement, before twirling around, now toasty warm. "Oh WOW. Your powers are amazing."

She laughed.

"Thanks." She said, grinning and I noticed that she had even made the clouds wonderfully fluffy, as if it were a glorious summer's day rather than a frosty winter. "It was getting far too cold out here for my liking, so I decided to do something about it."
I beamed at her.
"And you think my powers are 'oh so wonderful'?" I answered, looking at her in awe. "God. I'd love to have yours any day. Thinking about it," I added, "I'd ensure that England was permanently bathed in hot sunshine."

After my comment, Jasmine flashed me a smile, nodding in agreement. However, before she replied, her face somewhat darkened.
"You say that and yet, when I 'awakened', my powers were a nightmare to control. As soon as I experienced this change," she explained, "I created a storm over London, after finding out that I had failed my Science exam, nearly causing my teacher to be sucked into the core of a swirling hurricane!"

I laughed at hearing this statement, particularly as I remembered the weather report I had seen on the BBC news commenting on such a story.
It was still causing a buzz now.

Most meteorologists had stated that the whole incident was a freak occurrence of 'global warming'. Clearly, they had never heard of an 'awakening' before and the mind modification scouts had done their job properly.

Oblivious to my reminiscence, Jasmine continued on, unfazed.
"It was only through the help of my scout that I eventually managed to regain the upper hand. Also, this means that even now," she added, "I have to have complete focus in order to stop them from spiralling out of control."

As soon as she had finished talking, the humour of the situation dampened. I realised that she was speaking the truth. This was because I noticed that the sunlight was wavering and large grey clouds were beginning to form, high above our heads. Now, as I spoke, my voice had a faint uneasy tone to it.

"You're in control though right?" I asked her, a little apprehensive, as the clouds had proceeded to blot out the sun and were now going a darker black.

Throwing a glance in Jasmine's direction, I looked at her in alarm. I was unsettled by the tension in her face and frame.

"Jazz." I abruptly asked, my voice becoming agitated, as the light around us darkened even more. "Jazz...tell me that you have it all under control?"

Jasmine didn't answer me. Instead, she was frowning in concentration, the colours in her eyes going crazy.

"Jazz." I called to her again, as the clouds became seriously black. I thought I smelt the familiar smell of burning that accompanied a thunderstorm in the making. "JAZZ. ANSWER ME GOD DAMN IT!" I cried as the wind picked up and began to howl in my ears, whipping my hair against my face.

Jasmine didn't answer me. Flicking my eyes to hers, I was alarmed to see that the swirling, multi-coloured hue she had originally possessed was now replaced with a deep, coal black. I screamed again at her but, this time, the wind had picked up so much that it whipped my voice away.

I heard the hedges around us groan.

Dear lord, I realised, as I saw her frowning in effort and strain. She had lost control once more and, to make matters worse, I couldn't do anything to help her.

I was powerless.

Just before I thought I was going to be whisked away by the powerful winds hurtling around me, I heard Jasmine burst out laughing. She registered my petrified expression and the weather immediately returned to normal.
It was almost as if it hadn't changed.

When I had regained control of my pounding heart, I threw her a furious look.
"Don't ever do that to me again." I snapped, not seeing the amusing side of the situation. I breathed out a sigh of relief. "I genuinely thought that your powers had got the better of you and I was going to be swept away."

Jasmine looked wounded at my accusation, as I glared at her. However, despite my fury, I was pleased to see that her eyes had once again returned to their lighter shade of grey and not the scary black they had been a few moments ago.
"Aw Alex." She eventually said, helping me to my feet, her beautiful eyes wide with hurt. "Don't be like that. I may have been shaky when I 'awakened', but my scout gave me some wonderful advice. I wanted to –"
"So I and everyone else who happened to be in this area were your guinea pigs?" I interrupted, scowling.
She looked crestfallen by my anger.

Suddenly, her eyes flashed in annoyance at my fury.
"Oh, lighten up." She snapped back, cross at the lack of faith I appeared to have in her. "Nothing bad was really going to happen to you or anyone else. I had it all under control...honest."

The moment she had finished, I threw her a disbelieving look and crossed my arms in protest. After a brief hesitation, I sighed in surrender. I didn't want to have a fall blown argument with her, mostly as we had only just met and she could turn out to be the only friend I would ever make here. I also realised that, if I had been in

her shoes, I would have wanted to use my powers to see if I could control them better, particularly if I had been given some really useful advice. Anyway, perhaps she had realised that I had been trying to control my powers previously, just before we had met and, after realising this, had become desperate to do the same?
Who could blame her for wanting to do that?

Realising that that I had been too harsh on her, I took her hand in mine, before pulling her towards the massive lake.
She threw me a surprised look.
"I thought that you were mad at me?" She asked, although she allowed me to lead her onwards.
I threw her a small, apologetic smile.
"I was," I replied, "but then I realised my reaction was unreasonable. At the end of the day, you only wanted to practise your powers and I can understand that completely. After all," I concluded, "I wanted to do the same earlier on, when we first met."

After she had heard my response, she looked at me thoughtfully, her eyes shining.
"Thank you for understanding." She finally said, smiling. "Although I'm sorry for scaring you. I didn't mean to."

As soon as Jasmine had finished, I pushed any leftover anger away. From that moment onwards, I vowed to have more faith in her and acknowledged my own weaknesses in being too hasty in judging peoples' actions. Dropping her hand and laughing, I raced off towards the lake, hearing Jasmine soon follow me in hot pursuit.
"Bet I can reach the lake before you." I shouted, grinning and running like a maniac. I heard Jasmine laugh behind me, as we hurtled towards the gleaming lake before us.
"I bet you can't." She cried.

To my astonishment, she overtook me. Clearly, she was a good runner. As we giggled all the way down to the lake, our hair flying out behind us, I realised that this was a start of a fantastic friendship.

CHAPTER 12: ALEX

We spent the remainder of the day, before we went to find out our roommates, by the lake, investigating its surroundings and eating a selection of sandwiches for lunch. In the centre of the lake was a small island, encircled by an assortment of tall and large trees. This island could be accessed by a collection of small boats, from canoes to rowing boats, tied to the jetty. This was unless, like the unpleasant girl who could fly, you could get there without needing any form of water-based transportation.

Before we surveyed the island, we walked around the entirety of the lake, which was bordered by a huge wood, resting on stone seats dotted at various checkpoints and watching the ducks and swans swim contentedly by. To be honest, by the time we had completed a full circle, I had forgotten about our previous argument and about the cold, for I was roasting in my thick jumper and multiple layers of socks.

When Jasmine and I eventually completed a full circle, we had bonded like two people who had known each other for years. Both of us were musical. She played the piano and guitar and I sung, as well as played the flute. To make each other laugh, we practised harmonies to popular songs and Jasmine, like me, revealed that she wanted to be a full-time author when she was older. Due to this growing closeness, I soon decided that I could ask her how she felt when she first learnt of her powers and her 'awakening'. She met my question with a small, embarrassed smile.

"Well…after my scout had helped me regain control of my powers, she told me about Vladimir's academy. Since I knew I had been responsible, as my 'awakening' was on such a big scale, I quickly accepted the truth. However," she added, her eyes going glassy.

Awakening

"The hardest part was leaving my parents the following morning. I didn't get a wink of sleep at all."

Jasmine wiped her eyes on her sleeve, as we watched a solitary swan swim past. "It took so much effort to say goodbye."

At hearing this response, I placed my hand over hers.
"I know how you feel." I said, trying to comfort her. "I spent my last night crying the whole time, so much so that I looked like a zombie in the morning." I threw her an encouraging smile. "Still, I'm just grateful that I met such a lovely friend so early on during my time here. I've always found it hard to make friends. Therefore, I count myself lucky."

Jasmine shot me a beaming grin at hearing this comment, her tears rapidly receding.
"Oh Alex, thank you so much." She said, smiling. "I'm so lucky to have met you too. At least I now know one friendly face out of the many that go here."
I nodded.
"Me too." I replied, before I eyeballed the line of rowing boats.

Jasmine saw my line of gaze and, at seeing her excited face, we decided to try one out. After a wobbly (if not slightly wet) start, we eventually reached the island. Once we had made sure that the boat was well and truly secure to the post on the jetty, we headed off amongst the trees. The island itself wasn't that big and soon, we realised that we were reaching its centre, despite the fact that the trees were more tightly packed together now, making visibility harder. The small clearing, arranged with several logs, rocks and a small bonfire in the middle, which wasn't lit, told us that we had finally found the islands midpoint.
We weren't alone.

Just as I stepped into the clearing, a stick snapped, causing me to curse loudly. 'Mystery boy' sharply spun around, startled at first.

As soon as he saw me, his face relaxed.

"Oh." He said, in a voice that was deep. "It's you."

Jasmine came up behind me as he spoke and, at hearing his response to our arrival, threw him a heated glare.

"What's that supposed to mean?" She retorted, looking at him in an affronted manner.

Immediately, he realised that his initial comment had sounded rude and he stood up, before walking over to us, shaking his head apologetically.

"Sorry." He apologised, grinning weakly and flushing slightly, as he caught my eye. "I didn't mean to upset you and I guess that came out wrong. It was just that I was worried that you were a teacher and I don't want to get into trouble, particularly as I've only just got here."

The moment he had finished, Jasmine and I threw each other an amused glance. Once the words had left my lips, his gaze burned into mine.

My heart fluttered.

"So...what were you doing?" I asked him, blushing at the intensity of his gaze but nonetheless intrigued.

Immediately, 'Mystery boy' smiled at me.

Gosh, I thought. *His smile was another thing that I could add to the mounting list of: 'Things that were exceedingly hot about 'Mystery boy''.*

Stop. A voice in my brain screamed at me. *Just stop. You need to get to know this guy more before you even begin to think like that. After all, he could turn out to be a lunatic, for looks can be deceiving as you well know. Therefore, you need to be careful and watch your guard!*

As much as it pained me, I mentally made my choice. Oblivious to my mental debate, 'Mystery boy' answered my question.

"Well..." he said, going a little red and bringing me back from my thoughts. He threw his hand back behind his head, before pulling lightly at his hair, causing me to go all soft inside. "I was kind of practising and I didn't know if we were allowed to."

Jasmine, after hearing his vague explanation, was baffled by this answer, much like I was. I was pleased when she relieved the both of us of our puzzlement.

"Practising what?" She asked, frowning.

'Mystery boy' beamed at her.

"I was practising my powers." He replied, virtually bouncing up and down on the balls of his feet. "This place is amazing for it, as it's got such an incredible energy and because less people will get hurt by what I can do."

Now, after hearing the last part of his response, I was interested in this guy even more. I could tell that Jasmine was too from her facial expression. (The green-eyed monster grumbled at this fact).

"What can you do?" I abruptly asked, ignoring the jealous twinges in my stomach. The moment I spoke, I could tell that I had said the right question, for 'Mystery boy's' face glowed in animation.

"I can show you if you like?" He said. However, almost immediately afterwards, he looked crestfallen and stopped jumping up and down, which was a relief because his energetic movements had begun to make me feel sick. "But I don't know if that's acceptable outside of lessons?"

Jasmine and I threw each other another amused smile, once my stomach had calmed down.

"Well," said Jasmine, "both Alex and I have practised our powers since getting here and we haven't been told off. Therefore, I suggest you go for it."

For some reason, as soon as Jasmine had finished, this news hit the jackpot. 'Mystery Boy' seemed to puff out his chest, as if trying to impress us and rolled up his long sleeves. Overall, he looked as if he was preparing for a magic act. Subsequently, he gestured at us to step back, resuming his vigorous movements, causing my stomach to groan in despair.

"OK...well, if you could move backwards ladies so you don't get injured, in case this goes a little wrong that would be helpful." 'Mystery boy' instructed, his golden eyes gleaming in excitement. "Then, prepare yourself for the demonstration of a lifetime."

Jasmine and I laughed at hearing this remark and at the guy's clear enthusiasm. To our amazement, we realised that he was indeed talented. Using nothing but his mind, 'Mystery boy' made the pile of medium sized logs, which made up the non-lit bonfire and the several rocks scattered here and there, float up in the air and hover, before rotating them different ways around the three of us. Finally, he allowed them to slowly fall back to earth and hit the ground with a thud.

When he had finished his display, Jasmine and I stood there open-mouthed.

He had gotten a whole lot hotter.

"WOW!" Jasmine exclaimed, smiling at him in admiration, once he had finished his impressive show. "Your power is telekinesis. That's so cool."

'Mystery boy' flashed Jasmine a grin, pleased to see that he had made such an impact.

"Sure is." He laughed, thrilled with our response and showing us his mark, which was black in colour, in the shape of a brain, with golden, lightning bolts shooting out of it. "And I just want to get better and better. One day," he said, beaming at us. "I want to be able to move gigantic objects, just with the power of thought, but that'll only come with practise and time because sometimes," he added,

Awakening

chuckling. "I can get a little too eager, causing things to get out of hand."

Jasmine and I nodded in agreement, laughing.

"Same." Jasmine replied. "One day I want to be able to change the weather, in super quick time, without things going wrong."

It was the turn of 'Mystery boy' to look at her in amazement.

"Your power's weather control?" He asked Jasmine, clearly impressed.

She nodded, blushing.

For some reason, his response to her powers and Jasmine's reaction once again caused the green-eyed monster to rear its head and start growling.

Guiltily, I pushed it aside.

"Yeah." She answered, smiling, her cheeks pink.

"Awesome!" 'Mystery boy' replied, before he remembered an event that had occurred previously. "So...were you the one responsible for that random change in weather earlier?" he suddenly asked, his eyes sparkling.

Jasmine reddened even more, embarrassed, but I could tell she was confident in her powers.

"Yeah...I was." She eventually replied.

At hearing this conformation, I saw 'Mystery boy' pause for a moment, before he whistled.

When he replied, his face was radiant.

"Damn...that's epic." He said, making her laugh. Subsequently, he broke eye contact with her and looked at me expectantly.

It was now that I felt like I wanted the ground to swallow me up. Next to me were two people who had amazing powers, which were far more remarkable than mine. At the end of the day, 'Mystery boy' could potentially move buildings if he wanted to and, in terms of Jasmine, she could create devastating natural disasters, if she ever

became that dark minded. All I could do though, on the other depressing hand, was bend water into shapes.
That was hardly "epic" or "cool".

I blushed, ashamed of what I had been bestowed with.
"I can control the element of water." I mumbled, speaking really quickly and hoping that 'Mystery boy' didn't hear me. I dared to meet his eyes.
Much to my surprise, he flashed me a beaming grin.
"Now that's uber impressive." He smiled, waving his hands vivaciously about. "So, one day, you might be able to control all this water in the lake?"

This comment caught me off guard. I hadn't considered that possibility, after comparing it to everyone else's. Realising where 'Mystery boy' was coming from, I was relieved to see that somehow, my talent might not be mediocre after all.
"Yeah." I said, now smiling and filled with a new sense of self-awareness. "Yeah, one day that could happen."

As soon as I had finished talking, 'Mystery boy' flashed me a smile. When we looked at each other, I felt the same rush that I had felt earlier on. I blushed. It was then that the three of us decided that we would head back to the academy to find out what dorms we were in and to meet our roommates.

As we walked back to the academy, we exchanged names. Eventually, it came to 'Mystery boy'.
"So...what's your name?" I asked him, as he kindly helped me into my rowing boat, supporting my weight.
The boat wobbled dangerously.

When I was sitting down and happy that the boat wasn't going to tip over, I looked at him once more and he winked at me.
I blushed again.

"I'd never thought you'd ask." He replied, chuckling at my beetroot features, before continuing. "My name's Raphael and I guess that now we've officially introduced ourselves, we can all be friends?"

As we pushed off the bank, once he had gotten into his own boat, which had been hidden by some rather large bulrushes and headed towards the other side of the lake, I exchanged glances with Jasmine.

She nodded an agreement, smiling.

"Sure." I ultimately replied, heart pounding. I grinned at Raphael in the boat next to me, gently splashing him with the oar and laughed at his surprised reaction. "Sure. Jazz and I would love that."

CHAPTER 13: ALEX

And so judgement day arrived. Before long, the time came for us to find out our new roommates. Raphael, Jasmine and I entered the academy through the gigantic, back doors, carved with symbols that I had never seen before but seemed to give off an almost protective and comforting feeling. Soon, we had reached 'The Grand Western Wing' where residence numbers and a list of roommates were flashing in gold writing, on an enormous board in the centre of the room.

Unfortunately, the board was crowded and this area was particularly overflowing, due to the swarms of people. Clearly, I realised, whilst the three of us had been busy, exploring the outside of the academy, many other new students had arrived during that time. Many were different nationalities and had gathered in an enormous throng to inspect their residential fate. I craned my neck to see if I could spot Jack standing with a group of scouts, near one of the doorways, but he was not there. Sighing in momentary disappointment, the three of us fought our way to the front of the board. All the while, my stomach was filled with butterflies.
What I saw caused me to dance.

Jasmine and I had been put together. When she realised this, we both looked at each other in delight, grinning. Then, I turned to Raphael.
He was frowning.
Sensing me looking at him, he met my concerned gaze.
"Do you know a Lucifer Taylor?" He asked me.
I shook my head.
"Sorry." I replied. "That name doesn't ring a bell."
He repeated the same question to Jasmine but her reply was also negative.

Eventually, he shrugged.

"Oh well." He said, smiling weakly. "I'm sure he's a great guy and I guess that I'll just have to try and not take his name in such a biblical way."

At hearing this remark, Jasmine and I laughed, before we once again fought our way through the crowd and headed towards our dorm, which was unfortunately up many stairs. For an exercise phobic like me, this was a killer. When we reached the dividing stairwell, right at the top of the academy, we parted ways, realising that the dormitories were split into male and female.

"Well...I guess that we'll see each other at dinner?" Raphael asked, grinning before adding: "that's if I'm still alive by then."

Once again, Jasmine and I laughed.

"Jazz and I wish you luck." I replied, smiling when I had finished chuckling. "Although I'm sure you'll be fine. At the end of the day, names aren't always associated with personalities."

He flashed me a small smile.

"I'll bear that comforting thought in mind when I first meet Lucifer." Raphael replied, grinning. "And I'll give you the low down at dinner but, for now, see you both later."

Once he had finished, Jasmine and I nodded, before we watched Raphael disappear around the corner of the stair way. Damn, that guy had a nice rear end. Then, we made our own way towards our dormitory, both of us greatly looking forward to seeing what our room had to offer.

CHAPTER 14: ALEX

When we initially entered our room, Jasmine and I actually gasped. It was a modest size and had two double beds, which consisted of a navy quilt, patterned with a ring of six different coloured stars (I later found out that this was the academy's emblem). Over on the far, right-hand side, there were two medium sized cabinets and two huge wardrobes, which were filled with our clothes. Also, by the window, which was oval shaped and looked out onto the enormous lake, there was a small desktop onto which the early evening sunlight shone. Finally, we had an en-suite, as well as a small sofa in the middle of the room. All of a sudden, Jasmine flung herself onto the sofa, laughing in excitement and happiness, after the two of us had taken this in.

"Wow Alex." She said, grinning at me, her eyes shining. "This place is great."

I laughed and joined her on the sofa, lounging against the soft cushions.

"I know." I replied smiling back. "It has everything we could ever want."

Immediately afterwards, I noticed a small pile of papers sitting on the desktop, one pile with my name on it and one with Jasmine's. I went over and picked mine up, before handing Jasmine's to her. Before long, I had deduced that the pile of papers contained a welcome letter from Vladimir himself, a rule list, a map of the academy (I was thrilled to see that the academy had a library, an area that Mrs Sampson had unfortunately not taken us to on her tour) as well as our timetable.

In terms of my timetable, it consisted of the same lesson each week, including subjects that were found in a "normal" academic school, such as English, Maths and Science. However, one class,

Awakening

which you would not find on an average timetable, but was emphasised on mine, as well as Jasmine's, was Power Control.

As soon as Jasmine registered this subject, her eyes lit up.
"Oh Alex. Power Control sounds amazing. I can't wait to have that lesson."

I nodded my head in agreement. I was also looking forward to Music, as this was one of my favourite subjects and I was ecstatic to see that Jasmine was in most of my classes. Soon, I was distracted from my excited thoughts when I read that I would have to undertake physical education (PE). To me, this subject sounded dreadful, although it really depended on what type of PE we would be doing. If it was swimming or netball then I was normally fine. However, if it was dance or gymnastics, then I would be as good as dead, for I had no sense of balance or coordination. There was no way that my body was built for gymnastics and I looked like a contorted scarecrow when I danced. David had even resulted to caution on the dance floor, after I had left him with a bruised cheek when I had attempted the 'Macarena' during our Year Nine disco. I was relieved that both subjects weren't terribly frequent.

After reading the rules, the pair of us then set about decorating our room and unpacking our cases, which seemed to go by relatively quickly. Soon, all that needed to be unpacked and put up were my posters. Benedict Cumberbatch, as 'Sherlock Holmes' and Ian Somerhalder, as 'Damon Salvatore', filled the walls of my side of the room, as well as a large 'Doctor Who' poster of David Tenant, much to Jasmine's amusement and approval. When I was finished, I turned to inspect her own posters.

Jasmine was more of an animal person. As a result of this fact, numerous smaller posters littered the cream walls of cute baby animals, especially dolphins. Even so, the main poster she had pinned to the wall, which was situated directly above her bed, was of a gigantic picture of Johnny Depp as 'Captain Jack Sparrow'. I hi-fived her, as he too was one of my favourite actors.

On account of this shared interest, Jasmine soon began telling me that she had bought the box set of 'Pirates of the Caribbean' with her, in case we had a television.

This news was met with my excited cry.

"Jazz...that's fantastic news." I beamed at her. "We have a TV in the living room and, providing we're not disturbing anyone, we could begin 'Curse of the Black Pearl' right now, before we head down for dinner."

I had barely finished speaking when Jasmine was up and raring to go, the DVD clutched tightly in her hand. We left our dorm room in a flurry of teenage excitement and laughter. As soon as I entered the living room, my happiness immediately disappeared.

CHAPTER 15: ALEX

The girl who could fly, who was called Vanessa Johnson, a deduction I made purely based on the conversation she was having with her new best friend Tiffany, looked back at me with a mixture of shock, disgust and anger. Then, she exploded like a bomb, her beautiful hair bouncing up and down as she raged.

"What in god's name are you doing here?" She shouted at me, pointing her perfect nail in my direction and looking thunderous. "I didn't see your name on our dorm list!"

Man, what was that girl's problem with me?

In response to her furious outburst, I glared back at her, trying to keep calm. I frantically thought of a decent response, whilst my brain tried to deal with this horrible shock.

Perhaps there'd been a serious misunderstanding in the room designation? I thought as she stared at me as if I were a piece of dirt on her shoe. *There better have been.*

"The same could be said for you." I eventually replied, crossing my arms and frowning. Then, realising that her attitude and behaviour towards me had been uncalled for from the onset, I sighed in irritation. "What have I done to make you hate me so much?" I asked. "At the end of the day, we've only just met."

As soon as I had finished, I saw Vanessa stiffen at my question. When she replied, her voice was filled with disdain.

"I don't have to answer that." She responded, throwing me a condescending glance. "How I feel about people is my business."

I threw her the same "are you kidding?" look that I had given Jack earlier, although this was slightly heavier. This look was also reflected in Jasmine's features.

"Well...you need to tell me what you think if I'm ever going to make sense of your reaction to my presence." I retorted. "It's just as much my business, as it is yours, for I've been on the constant receiving end of your clear dislike for me ever since I arrived here this morning."

After my cutting remark, Vanessa seemed to make a funny noise in the back of her throat, before she shot me another foul glare.
"What I say might offend you." She retorted, fixing me with her cold eyes.
I shrugged.
"Your reaction to my existence has already offended me on a number of occasions. Therefore, I might as well hear all of your excuses."

Again, Vanessa made the same peculiar noise in the back of her throat, before she fixed me with an unreadable stare. Eventually, shaking herself, as if she was a jewel encrusted bird ruffling up her feathers, she began her long speech.
"My reasons for not liking you are perfectly admirable." She began, looking at me with superiority in her features and her lip curling. "When you arrived this morning and I saw you covered in that disgusting gunk which, even after it had been removed, seemed only to heighten the fact that you're not blessed with approving features like my own and wearing those rags, which you have the nerve to call clothes, I couldn't believe my own eyes. Also," she added, "even from the way that you hold yourself, I can tell that your background is one that should never be associated with this academy." Vanessa paused briefly, as if trying to recover from severe shock and I watched how Tiffany looked up her in admiration. Unfortunately, she was not finished. "Sadly though, this nightmare must be true as you're still here. However, I just can't understand how someone as respectable as Vladimir could possible allow you into this academy, of all people. I mean…the whole thing is just….just…unbelievable."

Awakening

As soon as Vanessa had finalised her cutting speech, she met my gaze in detest, the swirling icy fire of maliciousness burning in her eyes. She awaited my reply. I could not form any words, for I had been completely and utterly balled over.

How could someone even have the gall to think like that? I thought. Clearly, Jessica Wademen, for all her horribleness, had nothing on this girl.

She was the queen of meanness.

The others in the room appeared surprised, although Tiffany looked as if she was going to drop to her feet and worship Vanessa until the ends of the Earth. When we all came hurtling back to reality, I saw Jasmine, who was shaking with tremendous rage, take a step forward. I held out my arm, holding her back.

She growled.

"Let me at her." She hissed, fists clenched. "No one should be allowed to talk like that to someone and get away with it, particularly if they're my friend."

I shot her a small smile, despite my pale complexion, pleased to hear that she was supporting me. When she saw the hurtling emotions in my eyes, Jasmine thankfully complied, although she grumbled slightly. Then, I spoke, my voice scarily calm for someone who had just undergone serious verbal brutality.

"So...let me get this right?" I eventually said, looking at her directly in the eye, my own unwavering. "The reasons why you despise me so much include the fact that you think that I'm ugly, that you believe I have no fashion sense whatsoever and that my family is disgraceful?"

Slowly, after I had finished, Vanessa nodded, her eyes blazing. Seeing her unfazed reaction, I swallowed, struggling to keep my cool, as this conformation only fuelled my fury. Nonetheless, for far too long I had let people like Jessica Wademen walk all over me.

I was not going to let history repeat itself.

As a result of this, I told her like it was.

"Then I'm sorry to break it to you, but I think you need some serious mental help!" I replied, causing Tiffany and the others to gasp in shock, as well as Jasmine to practically choke. At hearing this, I saw a vain in Vanessa's temple twitch. I pressed on, not giving her the chance to answer back. "What's more," I added, "I've got some additional news for you. For your information, my ancestors have been coming to this academy for a long time and some of them have inherited such remarkable talents that it would make you green with envy. Therefore," I added, now smiling, knowing I was holding the ace card. "I'm staying right here, whether you like it or not and, if you have a major problem with that, then go and sort it out with the psychiatric department." Subsequently, not giving her a chance to reply, as I watched Vanessa turn scarlet, swelling in rage, I motioned for Jasmine to follow me. "Let's go Jazz," I said, turning my back on Vanessa and, as I did so, I heard Vanessa suck in air loudly, on the brink of exploding like never before. "I've spoken my mind and I think that we should give Vanessa here time to mull over what I've said." Consequently, checking Jasmine was behind me, I left the room, not once looking back.

As we made our way to our dorm room, laughing and Jasmine comically mimicking Vanessa's furious reaction to my response, Vanessa's screams and curses of wrath against me, once we were out of sight, was, strangely, like music to my ears.

CHAPTER 16: ALEX

Jasmine and I were still chuckling about Vanessa's reaction when we went down to dinner. Truthfully, I was both proud and shocked by my ability to stand up to her, considering my past experiences. Perhaps my newly 'awoken' powers had also blessed me with a newly found confidence?
That was a possibility.

As soon as we entered the dining hall, we stopped talking, gazing around us in wonder. The walls were made of stone and fixed to them were old-fashioned lights, which gleamed in the semi-darkness. Furthermore, the same lights, but in bigger form, hung from the ceiling in groups of eight and then, dangling from these lights, was the most fantastic feature of the whole hall. Countless flags, all different colours and bearing different power marks, like the one on my hand, shimmered in an unseen breeze. These power marks looked almost alive, as the light from the ancient candles fell onto the soft silk. In the distance, I saw my mark, so life-like I thought that I made out the wave gently tumbling on an ocean current.

As I walked through the hall, either side of me were long tables where many students had already gathered and were waiting for dinner to be announced. They were also talking in hushed friendship groups about events that had passed or gossiping. It was Raphael who broke my trance, as he called the two of us over to where he was sitting.
Soon, we sat down either side of his frame.
"So...how's your roommate?" I asked him, grinning, occasionally glancing around the room to take in the unbelievable presence of such an enormous space.
Raphael laughed.

"You know what," he said, smiling. "For someone named Lucifer, I think that he's an alright guy."

"What makes you think that?" Jasmine asked him.

Again, Raphael chuckled, before he delivered his verdict.

"Well...you know the teenager who was part of our group when we first met - the one who was seriously ripped?"

Both Jasmine and I nodded.

"Yeah," I replied, "I remember him. He was the boy who constantly looked as if he was going to snap you in half any second. Is he Lucifer?"

Raphael nodded.

"Yeah, that's him." He answered. "Well, obviously strength's his power. He almost crushed my hand when we greeted each other. However, deep down, I think he's pretty decent."

I frowned.

"Why's that?" I asked. "He sure as hell gives off the opposite impression."

Raphael laughed once more, before speaking.

"Well...let's just say that I did a little snooping when he was in the shower earlier and I came across a *very* interesting leaflet amongst his stuff."

As soon as he had finished, my heart fluttered. The feelings of excitement and anticipation flooded through my veins, before another weird emotion encompassed me. It was the kind of sensation you get just before secrets are laid bare – secrets that are supposed to be kept hidden. Raphael lowered his voice, grinning like a naughty child, before he looked around to see that no one was listening in. Seeing that the coast was clear, he revealed all.

"I believe that secretly, Lucifer's a right softy at heart, for the leaflet was all about the RSPCA."

Awakening

At hearing this news, Jasmine and I exchanged amazed glances. From Lucifer's bulky physique and powerful presence, I couldn't get my head around what Raphael was saying.

"No way." I replied. "There must be a mistake. No way does he look like the kind of person who enjoys cuddling and helping cute cats and dogs. He's more likely to crush them instead with his huge hands."

Raphael shrugged.

"I'm just relating what I saw."

I was about to continue in my amazement when the sound of sharp clapping could be heard. The clapping came from the high table at the end of the hall. It was Mrs Sampson (who I later found out taught Citizenship) and, every head, including mine, turned in her direction. Before long, all students within the room, including me, began to join Mrs Sampson as the other professors of the academy and the headmaster entered the hall. Ultimately, they reached their individual seats and sat down.

As soon as my eyes had rested on the elegantly decorated, high table, I scanned each face in turn. In the far-left hand corner was a man who had a stern expression, matted, damp hair and sharp, blue eyes. Next to him was a woman with soft features, dressed in a blue and yellow flowery dress, with a red hair band and short, raven hair. (Due to her soft features and dress style, she reminded me of 'Snow White').

Alongside her was Mrs Sampson and then, to her right, sitting in a large, intricate, carved chair, was the oldest man in the room. He had unfathomable eyes and wore a very thoughtful and profound expression. Immediately, I recognised him as being the almighty Vladimir Alcaeus and I actually shook in excitement and awe as I studied his features. He seemed to ooze power and authority, despite his age.

Moving on, I flicked my gaze to the stern person sitting the other side of him. She was an older woman with sharp, severe features and the build of an ox. By studying her, my guess was that she taught PE. Therefore, I realised, especially because of her powerful build, that I better not get on the wrong side of her or so help me god. All the same, the person sitting beside ox woman couldn't have been more opposite in size and appearance and I actually laughed silently to myself, imagining them as a comedy double act.

This person was a young man who could only have been a few years older than Jack. He was very slim and he gave off a calm quality about him, as he gazed pensively around the hall with a relaxed interest. As I flicked my eyes casually back to my fellow students, I could immediately tell he was the hot favourite amongst the females, who were all admiring him with dreamy expressions. Nevertheless, out of the professors who sat upon that table, it was the final woman who interested me the most.

This woman was also young, around the same age as the dreamboat professor sitting to her right. She was stunningly beautiful, although this wasn't in the normal sense, for she had an unusualness about her looks and was dressed like a gothic angel, which was emphasised by her long, lacy, black dress. Much like the adoring female fans who fawned over the young male professor, many of the males, including Raphael, studded her with equally wistful glances, causing surprisingly envious emotions to rise in the pit of my stomach. Finally, this professor had long, snow-white hair which fell to her waist, something that heightened her seriously pale complexion and possessed sharp, icy blue eyes. It was these eyes which, once they met mine, caused my body to jolt unpleasantly.

As soon as our gazes locked, I felt as if I had been punched in the stomach by an icy hand and my body began to shiver and twitch uncontrollably. As much as I tried too, I felt powerless to break the spell she had over me. Gradually, as the connection lengthened, I soon began to feel ill. I felt as if she was searching my very existence. It was Mrs Sampson who saved me.

Just before I felt like I was going to be violently sick then and there, in front of the whole academy, Mrs Sampson began to speak. Instantly, as if it had never happened, the sickness vanished.
The hold she had over me was broken.

As soon as it was gone, I refused to meet the mysterious woman's gaze again, although I could feel her eyes boring into the side of my face, willing me to look at her once more. After a few moments, I felt her gaze lift, for she now fixed it on a talkative Mrs Sampson. Inwardly, I breathed out a sigh of relief. Then, taking a deep breath to calm my pounding heart and rocketing stomach, I fixed my gaze permanently on Mrs Sampson, now listening to what she had to say.
"That's better." She exclaimed, once the whispered mutterings had stopped, not long after she had finished clapping. After a few moments, I realised that her voice was far louder than it had been when we first met, as it now appeared to carry into every nook and cranny of the hall. Therefore, I realised that she had the power of sonic voice, which was AWESOME.
Her words brought me back to reality.
"Now," she continued, "the headmaster of the academy would like to say a few words, before we start eating. And so, please bring your hands together once again, in a round of applause, for the incredible and highly respected Vladimir Alcaeus."

As soon as his name had been announced, Vladimir rose with an authoritative grace, before acknowledging all with a short, curt nod. Then, he addressed everyone in a voice that was filled with a powerful resonance.

"Thank you Mrs Sampson for your kind words." Vladimir began, his eyes swirling with many colours and he threw us a delighted beam. "And thank you all for working so hard each and every day on your studies, as well as on your more mystical talents (his eyes suddenly flashed gold, as if to emphasise his point and I, along with everyone who sat closest to the high table, gasped in amazement). I say this because I've heard many positive reports, over the past few weeks, saying that your commitment to and enthusiasm for each lesson has been fantastic."

Once Vladimir had finished this introduction, he paused momentarily, to allow people to clap again. When the clapping had died away, after he raised his wizened hand for silence, he continued on with his speech, his eyes twinkling with a thousand emotions.

"However, as I scan the faces of each and every one of you, I notice that there are many new ones, who I do not recognise amongst my students. Consequently, I send a warm welcome to those who are about to start this academy, as a result of your 'awakening' and I hope that your journey here was problems free."

As soon as Vladimir mentioned the "problems free" journey, I had to bite back a retort. All the same, as I watched Vladimir pause once again, his bushy eyebrows raised high in his thin face as he spoke, I realised that somehow, I really did feel at home here.

"This change," Vladimir stated, "I assure you, will be hard. Nonetheless, I hope that your time at my academy will also be filled with fun and laughter. After all, it's not every day that you come across a school filled with students who possess amazing powers and who may, one day, be the next 'Hulk' or 'Wonder Woman'."

At this last comment, students and teachers alike laughed. Even the mysterious gothic woman with the cold eyes allowed herself to smile.

Then, Vladimir wrapped up his speech.

"Therefore, with the wonderful food we're about to consume and the raising of my glass, I wish you all good luck, from the bottom of my heart."

On cue, as Vladimir raised his glass in a toast, a solitary waiter arrived out of a side door. To my amazement and delight, he duplicated himself until he and his countless doubles were able to carry the mountains of delicious food, prepared by his hand, to all the long tables. The doubles also visited the high table and Vladimir Alcaeus met them with a warm smile and a kind word of thanks. Subsequently, when they were done, the feast began.

To be honest, there was so much food to choose from that I was overwhelmed. After much debating, I settled on a few of my favourite dishes – tomato soup and bread for starters, lasagna and vegetables for my main course and hot, chocolate fudge cake for pudding. Raphael didn't seem to have such a problem, a fact emphasised by the childish gleam in his golden eyes. He seemed to try as much of the food around him as he could, even the more exotic looking cuisine.

After much eating and laughing and an eventual terrible stomach ache, we were soon filing out of the hall and off to bed, the knowledge that the next day was going to be filled with much confusion, hard work and excitement. As I left the hall, pleased to see that Vanessa was nowhere in sight, I felt the ever-lingering presence of two, freezing, sapphire eyes, which followed me all the way up the marble stairs, until I was out of sight.

It was these eyes that haunted my dreams.

CHAPTER 17: HECATE

"Vladimir!" Hecate's sharp voice floated down the hallway.

At the sound of his name, Vladimir spun around abruptly, resulting in a flurry of sparks to be released from his fingertips. He paused to allow for his esteemed, young professor to catch up.

"Yes Hecate." He asked as soon she had approached, frowning in interest and confusion. Vladimir sensed something of importance was weighing heavily on her mind. "What's the matter?"

When Hecate was standing directly in front of him, her black, lace dress swishing about her feet, she began to speak.

"I know you're very busy and you've got plans for this evening, but can I talk to you for a moment please?" Hecate asked him, her voice betraying a sense of excitement, which was a rarity in her book, for she was usually calm and distant. "I've something very important to say."

At hearing her intriguing comment, Vladimir straightened, making himself taller.

He cleared his throat before speaking.

"Certainly." He replied. "You know that I'd always listen to anything you wish to say. After all, you'll forever have my upmost respect. Therefore, without further ado, I'm all ears."

Slowly, smiling softly, Hecate revealed her exciting news, although she still had that ever lingering bite to her words.

"Well." She began, swallowing to calm her breathing. "I strongly believe that one of the new students, who arrived today, has the potential to possess outstanding talents."

At hearing this information, Vladimir's heart began to pound and the silence lengthened considerably, before he eventually found his voice.

He could barely get the words out.

Awakening

"W...when you say that this student: 'has the potential to possess outstanding talents'." Vladimir echoed slowly, shaking with anticipation at the wonderful thoughts that were racing around his mind. "Do you mean to say that these talents are beyond average?" Slowly, Hecate nodded.

"Yes." She replied. "When we were sitting at the high table during dinner, I started to undertake my regular scanning of the room, just like you requested me to do and, whilst I was doing this, one of the new students, a girl, met my gaze."

Hecate paused to collect her swirling thoughts.
Eventually, she continued.

"When she did." She gradually answered, her eyes wide. "I experienced a sensation like I've never felt before."

Hecate paused briefly, shivering as she recalled the sheer power she had felt lurking within that one frame. It had made her, Hecate, with her own incredible powers, feel insignificant in comparison. She could not shake that unbelievable sensation, when the two of them had been connected.

At seeing Hecate's clear emotional state, Vladimir shivered, stunned that someone had the ability to affect Hecate so much, when so many others had failed. A small bright light of hope sparked within him.

"H...Hecate..." Vladimir began cautiously, but he had to stop for a moment in fear of collapsing under the monumental feeling of hope. Sooner or later, he found the ability to speak. He had wanted to say these words for so long. "D...do you think that you've possibly found someone who may provide a solution to our problems?"

Hecate thought for a moment before speaking.

"Maybe." Hecate replied, a small smile playing about her lips. "But we should wait a while in order to clarify that my suspicions are correct. I'm still debating whether this task should be undertaken by a soul individual. After all, one person on their own may be able to save the world. However, a team of friends, all working together, have a much greater chance of succeeding...providing that no one succumbs to evil."

Vladimir felt as if he could burst. Nonetheless, as he hastily looked about him, hoping that no one had overheard their private conversation, he realised that he must keep his excitement to a minimum. After all, Hecate was right. They had to wait and see if her suspicions were correct. Then, if they were, he could take matters from there.

"Well done Hecate." Vladimir finally said. "All that planning has hopefully paid off. Originally, I thought our odds at defeating Mortimer were bordering on zero. Now though," he continued, "it looks like we might have a chance. Still," he concluded, calming himself to some degree. "I'd like to put you in charge of tracking this student and confirming your thoughts. Only then, when this has been established, can we take the whole business one step further."

With a curt nod, Hecate accepted her assignment, before she gradually began to part ways with the headmaster. She hadn't gone far when Vladimir called her back.

"Oh, and Hecate?" He cried, halting her for a moment. "I'd like to keep this news to ourselves."

Once more, Hecate nodded. Then, the two of them parted in the surrounding darkness.

CHAPTER 18: ALEX

My first lesson was Music and, all in all, it was amazing. Ironically, but nonetheless undeniably awesome, I found out that my music teacher was called Miss Crotchet. Her power included the ability to communicate with animals, exactly like my great grandfather - Alistair. She initially demonstrated her power at the beginning of the lesson by singing a recognisable tune — Lady Gaga's 'Edge of Glory'. Much to my delight and that of the class, her singing meant that a flock of doves, which had been roosting in the academy's rafters, flew through the classroom window, landed on the teacher's desk and replied to her song with beautiful trills. Therefore, I firmly concluded that she was more or less a real-life version of the Disney princess 'Snow White'.

During the lesson, Miss Crotchet told us that we would be studying one, famous composer each week, starting with Mozart. She also explained to us that we would be looking, listening and trying to replicate some of his works, but putting our own stamp on it. This announcement was met with excitement from everyone, especially from Lucifer. Although he was subtler about his interest, he betrayed his keen curiosity through his body language, which I found surprising. For now though, I focused on the lesson at hand.

The whole lesson started with listening to sections of 'The Magic Flute' by Mozart, as well as enjoying listening to Miss Crotchet attempt some difficult parts. Then, we set to work on the computers, hoping to create a recognisable, catchy melody that Mozart was renowned for. Lucifer evidently excelled in this assignment. Miss Crotchet had just finished talking to Jasmine when she went and sat down next to him, before she put the headphones onto her head, eagerly looking forward to hearing his work so far. She was not disappointed. It was her high-pitched shriek of delight, combined with an incredible display of his melody, which told us Lucifer was an undiscovered talent at composition.

"Oh, wow Lucifer." Miss Crotchet gushed, beaming at him in amazement and excitement, as she patted him hardly on his broad back. (Due to his muscular form, her pats probably felt like gentle taps to him). "Your solo melody is incredible. Plus," she added, "you've even managed to add some counterparts and harmony in the strings, woodwind and brass. Clearly, you're a mastermind of a composer!"

After this dramatic display of excitement, Lucifer, in all his hefty bulk, turned bright red, blushing in embarrassment.

"Thanks..." He just about forced himself to mumble, before he buried himself back within the music, trying to hide his burning features.

Jasmine and I exchanged intrigued glances, before we set about continuing with our work. I was pleased when Miss Crotchet came over to me and praised me for my own musical talents, for I wasn't that bad at composing (modesty is my speciality). Nevertheless, just as the bell went for second period and I watched Lucifer hurry out of the room as quickly as possible, still self-conscious, Miss Crotchet called me aside.

At first, I was a bit surprised and nervous by this request, for I feared that I might have done something wrong. Still, calming these unwelcome sentiments, I motioned for Jasmine to leave me and mouthed that I would meet her in PE. Once Jasmine had disappeared, Miss Crotchet continued.

As she spoke, my anxiety evaporated.

"I just wanted to talk to you about your great grandfather - Alistair Silverstone." Miss Crotchet explained to me, smiling kindly. "It's a real pleasure to be able to teach one of his successors. After all," she added, "as you can imagine, he was a great inspiration of mine."

Awakening

After she had finished, I let out a sigh of relief.
"Thanks." I replied, returning her smile. "To be honest, I've only just found out about Alistair on my birthday, although I'll say that the whole story of his 'awakening' made me laugh."
At hearing my words, Miss Crotchet chuckled.
"I know." She said, grinning. "I remember reading that tale when I was looking through his file in the library. He was quite a character you know."
After hearing her last comment, I threw Miss Crotchet an interested and intrigued look, before I asked the question lurking in my mind.
"You don't suppose that I could have a look at his file?" I enquired, hoping that, as she clearly had a lot of respect for my great grandfather, she would be willing to grant me my request.
At first, Miss Crotchet looked uncertain. All the same, at the last second, she changed her mind.
"I don't see why not. Really, students are prohibited from accessing the files, unless they're for an assignment. Nevertheless, I suppose I can make an exception in your case."
I threw her a thankful smile.
"Thanks." I replied, beaming up at her. "I promise that I'll only examine the one file."
Miss Crotchet nodded her head.
"Very well then." She said, smiling. "Next time we have music, I'll give you my permission and I'm sure you'll thoroughly enjoy reading about your famous, family ancestor. I know I did."
After we had finalised the agreement, I bid her goodbye and thanked her once more. Then, I set off towards the bane of my subject life - PE.

CHAPTER 19: ALEX

PE or otherwise known as physical education. This word was comprised of two single letters, which would normally not cause anyone any trouble. They were two single letters that were usually associated with the further words of "health" and "extended life" and therefore, had a positive reputation. However, for me, the P and the E put together was the worst possible combination. Every time they were mentioned, I would sigh in displeasure, my heart rate would increase and I would feel lightheaded. After all, in my mind, PE = exercise and exercise = torture!

As I approached the changing room and smelt the vile stench of sweaty bodies, unhappiness began to kick in. On cue, my heart started to beat faster and I felt as if I was about to be sick. Jasmine saved me at the last second by poking her head around the door, before I thought I was going to faint.

However, she was not the bearer of good news.

"Alex - you need to hurry up and get changed." She said quickly, her face paling. "I tried to reason with our new PE teacher but she isn't taking: 'Alex needed to stay behind and talk to our Music teacher' as an acceptable excuse to be late to this class."

"Too right she isn't!" Suddenly shouted a deep, booming voice from behind me. As soon as this sharp, harsh voice met my ears, I nearly jumped out of my skin at the fierceness of the sound. "You girl need to get a move on if you want to avoid having a detention on your first PE lesson."

Hastily spinning around, my shocked gaze met the fearsome sight of my teacher nemesis. She was now standing directly in front of me, inches from my own feeble form and flexing her bulging muscles in a threatening manner. She fixed me with a heated stare.

Awakening

Great! I thought, inwardly groaning and wishing that I could be absorbed into the floor. *We had ox woman as our PE instructor.* She had more hair on her upper lip than 'Chewbacca' had on his entire body!
I shuddered.
"Well don't just stand there, gawking at my beautiful self." Ox woman abruptly roared, as I lost all sense of communication, making me jump again, so much so that I almost leapt right through the changing room roof. "Get cracking."

Instantly, after this bark of a command, I bounded into action, practically throwing my PE clothes onto my quivering body. As I changed into my PE kit, faster than a 'Quick change' act, I became ever fearful of having a detention, let alone receiving potential broken bones all over my body if I didn't manage to get ready on time. One punch from those bone-crushing fists would surely leave me in hospital for well over a month. I must have set a record pace by the time I stood ready to be put through hell. Grunting and muttering silent curses under my breath, I prayed that the type of PE we were about to endure was something I could just about cope with.

After smiling at me, or more grimacing, ox woman turned her fierce expression onto the whole class.
"So...girlies (she mustered up as much sarcasm as she could) now that all of us are ready (she threw me a particularly unpleasant glare) I feel that it is my duty to inform you of my name and what we're actually doing in PE today."

Ox woman's thick, rubbery lips peeled back to reveal a set of humongous teeth, before she continued.
"My name is Miss Beast (I actually had to stop myself from choking on my water bottle at this revelation) and I've decided that we will be attempting Netball today. Therefore," she concluded, "I'm hoping

that at least some of you possess the ability to throw a ball properly and if I hear one whiny comment about breaking a nail, then so...help....you...god."

After she had threatened us and had clicked her knuckles hostilely, no one spoke for fear of being reprimanded, even if I did see a few of the girls quickly look at their perfect nails and grimace. Still, turning abruptly on her heal, Miss Beast marched us out of the changing rooms and into the huge sports hall.

As soon as Miss Beast had finished handing out our bibs and explained the rules of the game, she motioned for us to go to our positions. Whilst we sluggishly moved, she mentioned one other rule that wasn't on the normal list.

"Oh, and one more thing." Miss Beast added. "No one – I mean no one, is allowed to use their powers for help throughout the entirety of the game, or they'll have me to deal with. Do I make myself clear?"

After hearing this last threat, all of us nodded, swallowing.

Then, the game began.

Slowly, I jogged over to my start position on one of the yellow lines, for I was playing the position of Goal Attack. This meant that I was in charge of getting the ball into the net, although I still needed to help my team against the other players. As I sussed out the defence, my heart sunk. There, playing Goal Keeper, someone who would be preventing me from scoring a goal and was set about making this game as lethal as possible, in my respects, was Vanessa. As soon as our eyes made contact, she scowled at me. I saw rage burning in her eyes. Therefore, sighing, I knew that this was not going to be a simple and easy match. However, I decided that I would cross that hurdle when I came to it.

Before I knew it, the whistle to signify the start of the game had been blown. Game on. I was on high alert. Not long into the game, I

Awakening

relaxed. Soon, I had switched off all interest in the matter completely. The bulk of the game went by so...painfully...slowly. This was because the majority of my team were clearly terrible at Netball and I will add that this was almost certainly because most of them were afraid of any harm coming to their beloved nails.

As a result of the appalling lack of enthusiasm and skill, Miss Beast would often go beetroot red and shout unthinkable threats to members of my team – threats that could, in some cases, borderline on obscene. Nevertheless, mercifully, right towards the end of the match, this sluggish atmosphere changed.

"Alex – catch." Jasmine's voice rang about the gym.

As if I had been struck by lightning, my head shot up and met the joyful sight of the ball hurtling towards me. As soon as it had made contact with my hands, I acknowledged that the game for my team had finally begun. Turning sharply around on my heel, I threw the ball back to Jasmine who was playing Centre. Luckily, she caught it just before the opposition could stop her.

Then, I entered the shooting area.

I came face to face with my archenemy.

"You're going down!" Vanessa snarled at me, her eyes flashing, as they met mine.

"Not if I can help it." I retorted back before I nodded to Jasmine to pass me the ball.

In a flash, the ball came hurtling my way and I ducked under Vanessa's flailing arms. Much to my delight, the ball touched my fingers and I pulled it against my chest, claiming it as if it was the most important object in the world. This was not before I cried out in pain, as Vanessa's perfect fingernails caught my skin, clawing down my hands like vicious talons and leaving bloody trails across my bare flesh. She smirked when she noticed her handiwork and I threw her a heated glare filled with venom, wincing as my hands stung. Even so, as I positioned myself to take the first and only shot of the game for my team, I forgot her temporarily and focused on the hoop. Taking a deep breath and muttering a prayer, I threw it towards the post.

At first, my team mates let out an excited cheer, as it looked like it was going to be a fantastic goal – our only goal. However, as soon as I had thrown the ball, our joy was blotted out by Vanessa's tanned hand. I watched in despair as her fingers touched the ball, before she knocked it off its desired path. Furthermore, where one favourable path had been ruined, another was made. The ball came hurtling off course and straight into the side of my head.

I collapsed onto the floor in agony.

Whilst I groaned and saw stars, I felt what was going to be one heck of a bruise begin to form. Through the pain, I could faintly make out what sounded like an explosive argument happening nearby.

"She used her powers." I heard Jasmine raging. Painfully opening my eyes and clutching my head, I saw the drama unfold. "She used her powers to gain the extra height she needed to stop that ball and then made sure it hit Alex!"

Slowly, I noticed that Miss Beast had called the game to a halt the moment I had been hurt. She now stood between Jasmine and Vanessa, preventing them from clawing out each other's eyes and listening to what the two of them had to say in weighty silence.

"Nonsense." Vanessa retorted, flicking a loose strand of golden hair off her face angrily. "As if I'd do something like that. It was simply an accident."

Jasmine threw her a venomous glare.

"What a load of crap." Jasmine swore, pointing her finger at Vanessa. "I know you did that on purpose. After all, you made it very clear yesterday that you despise Alex and therefore, you played dirty."

Awakening

I noticed how Vanessa's eyes narrowed.

Suddenly, she flung herself forward.

"Why you —" Vanessa retorted.

Before she could finish speaking, Miss Beast had heard enough. She pulled Vanessa back with such strength that she was almost thrown over to the other side of the hall.

Then, she let rip.

"SILENCE!" Miss Beast shouted, fixing both Jasmine and Vanessa with a warning look, filled with fury. "Why…the two of you argue like an old married couple."

Then, she fixed her attention onto me.

I softly moaned in pain and, at seeing my agony, she closed the gap between the two of us in a matter of seconds, thanks to her gigantic strides.

"Now." She looked at me, checking me all over. "I think that you need to go to the nurse."

No shit Sherlock. I thought back, as the pain doubled ten-fold.

All the same, as soon as she had finished, she picked me up as if I were no lighter than a feather, squishing me against her bulky, sweaty body and causing me to prevent myself from gagging. Perhaps she had heard me and this was my punishment?

She sharply turned back to Vanessa and Jasmine.

"As for you two, I'll deal with you later." She growled. Subsequently, Miss Beast walked out of the sports hall, with me wincing in tow, praying that her beloved gym would not become a war zone in the time that she was absent.

CHAPTER 20: ALEX

The nurse was lovely, although she was spoken to rather gruffly by Miss Beast, as she entered the room. However, I realised that Miss Beast seemed to be someone who was always talking to people in an unfriendly way. Consequently, as if it were nothing new, the nurse met her arrival with nonchalance.
"I've got a pupil for you Mrs Frost." Miss Beast said curtly, placing me down on one of the medical tables rather harshly. "She's got a nasty injury to the side of her head."

As soon as her name was called, Mrs Frost was by my side in a flash. She had greyish hair, a petite form and bright, kind blue eyes.
"Oh dear, you poor thing." She said, wincing as she saw my bruise. "That looks very unpleasant." She turned to Miss Beast. "Thank you, Louise, for bringing her here. She needs urgent medical attention, as head wounds can be serious."

The instant Mrs Frost had said Miss Beast's first name, I was taken aback by how soft it sounded. Miss Beast was a woman with such a strong, powerful build and dominant personality that her first name didn't sound right. All the same, Miss Beast nodded sharply, before she turned to leave.
Mrs Frost wasn't done talking.
"Oh, and Louise." She continued, smiling softly. "I've got your special medicine with me - you know the one that helps you control your temper, if you would like to collect it? I finished making it last night."

After Mrs Frost had finished, I noticed how Miss Beast looked as if she wanted to crush the nurse with her little finger. Eventually, she muttered a gruff thanks under her breath, nodding. Nevertheless, that didn't stop her from meeting my eyes with a gaze that said: "If you ever breathe a word of this to anyone, I'll hunt you down and smash you into pieces." I stayed silent whilst Mrs Frost dealt with

Awakening

her fellow staff member, before Miss Beast really did leave, much to my relief. Subsequently, I was left to be attended by the delicate hands of Mrs Frost.

As soon as Miss Beast was gone, Mrs Frost set about inspecting my bruise.

"Quite a bump that is." She muttered before she hurried away and came back with a small, empty, plastic bag. "Let me deal with it immediately."

As if on cue, the magic began. Once she had the bag clutched tightly in her hand, I watched how it suddenly became very cold within the room until, to my amazement, the bag began to fill with ice.

I let out a small cry of wonder.

"Wow." I breathed out slowly. "You have ice powers!" After she had finished making the ice pack, she motioned to me to put in on my head. "And there was me thinking that you would have healing powers, being the academy's nurse?"

Slowly, Mrs Frost smiled at my clear astonishment.

"I often get that reaction." She grinned, her blue eyes flashing in delight and amusement. "And I suppose it would make more sense," she continued. "After all, people would be healed at a quicker rate if it were so. However," she added, "in my opinion, my powers being what they are keeps things interesting, in addition to the fact that I'm pretty hot on my medicines and remedies."

I couldn't help but laugh as I heard Mrs Frost's argument as to why she should be allowed to keep her job. Clearly, Vladimir didn't have any objections with her work, as I was sure that she had been at the academy for quite a long time.

After I had finished laughing, I decided to reveal my own talent.

"I suppose your power's similar to mine," I told Mrs Frost, "as I can control the element of water."

At hearing this snippet of information, Mrs Frost's eyebrows raised in intrigue.

"Well...that's an interesting talent. We've had air, fire and earth benders at this academy, but we've never had a water bender. I don't know why that is."

As soon as I heard this revelation, my stomach tightened in excitement and surprise. This was an amazing fact and it shocked me to think that I was presently one of a rare kind. Still, I was pleased to hear that there were fellow students, at this academy, who could control an element like me. Mrs Frost brought me back to reality, as she handed me my medication.

"This bottle and small bag contain paracetamol, a special medicine that was made by my own two hands and ice packs." She explained. "In a few days, if you take the medicine regularly, the bruise should be gone. However," she finalised, "for now, if you would like to have a sleep in the medical beds over in the other room, up until lunchtime, you're more than welcome."

I thanked her profusely, which she waved off with her hand. After deciding to try and have a nap, as I came over feeling somewhat nauseous, I was just about to fall asleep when I heard the rustling of clothes. Instantly, the temperature in the room dropped and I knew that it wasn't Mrs Frost's doing.

No.

Instead, it was the fault of someone else. Turning over as if to make it look like I was sleeping, I kept my eyes closed, although I ensured that I could still see what was going on through the gap in my eyelashes. My heart dropped. Standing a few feet away from my table was the mysterious woman with the cold eyes. I felt her icy stare searching mine out, even though she assumed I was asleep. I found it hard not to open my eyes. Soon, the mysterious woman pulled her attention away from me and set about talking to Mrs Frost, who clearly was as unnerved as I was.

"H...H...Hecate." Mrs Frost stammered and immediately, my blood ran cold. I realised that the mystifying woman's name couldn't have suited her more. It was another name to add to the growing list titled: 'Fitting first names', which included Miss Beast. "I...I didn't expect to see you here. Is there a particular reason as to why you've visited my ward?"

Slowly, Hecate once more flicked her gaze onto me before she spoke, her voice as freezing as her eyes.

"As a matter of fact, there is Linda." Hecate said, every word emphasised. "I've come here with regards to a particular subject of interest and, rather conveniently, it's to do with the girl you've just been dealing with."

At hearing this comment, my heart rate increased and I became fearful that I would give myself away. However, managing to stay as calm and collected as I could, I pushed down my mounting terror and concentrated on listening to what Hecate had to say. After listening to Hecate, Mrs Frost made a strange noise in the back of her throat - a similar noise to the one Vanessa had made previously. Nevertheless, knowing what Hecate was capable of, she answered her.

"What is it that you want to know?" Mrs Frost asked, frowning slightly in confusion and concern on my behalf.

Hecate merely ignored her.

"Firstly, what's the girl's name?" She asked, looking around for a medical record.

Mrs Frost didn't need to get mine out, for she already knew the details after dealing with my injuries.

"Alexandra." Mrs Frost replied, a little too quickly for her liking, although she put it down to Hecate's presence. "Her name's Alexandra Raven."

At hearing this clarification, Hecate let out a sigh. It was almost as if this news had released her of a troublesome thought.
"And what's the nature of her powers?" Hecate further enquired.

At hearing this question, Mrs Frost paused, now becoming unsettled by this interrogation. All the same, it was as if Hecate had an unspoken power over her and, against any doubts, she revealed all.
"She's an elemental controller." Mrs Frost explained, swallowing uncomfortably. "More specifically, she can control the element of water."

Once again, Hecate seemed to emit sentiments of relief and even some surprise at this answer. Thankfully though, the questioning was over...for now.
"See to it that Alexandra gets the maximum rest." Hecate abruptly demanded, making Mrs Frost jump, as she directed her pale hand towards the "sleeping" me. "And the best medical care. After all, that bruise she's received looks positively awful." She turned to go. Realising that she had forgotten something, she added in a final comment. "Oh, and lastly Linda, when Alexandra awakens, tell her that all of her clothes, books and belongings are back in her dorm room. I sent a few members of staff to collect them when I found out what had happened to her." Then, without another word and with one last look at me, Hecate was gone in a swirl of black lace.
The temperature of the room resumed its previous level.

After she was gone, I heard Mrs Frost breathe out. Clearly, she had been worried that she was about to experience more of Hecate's unusual behaviour and questioning. As my mind raced with a thousand thoughts, I noticed the concern in her eyes. She gazed at me in a way that unnerved me. After all, it was a well-known fact that anyone who interested Hecate would end up experiencing a dark fate. It was also common knowledge, on an even more sinister note, that the person of interest could more or less, one day, in whatever shape, way or form, end up as good as dead.

CHAPTER 21: ALEX

The next few hours went by painfully slowly. I was kept awake by a constant stream of confused thoughts regarding what had just passed and what I had just witnessed. Nevertheless, I still felt comfortable on the medical bed and was able to have the odd nap now and again. For that reason, I stayed where I was. When I realised it was time for lunch, as soon as I smelt the delicious food coming from the dining hall, I shakily got to my feet and thanked Mrs Frost. She met my thanks with a small smile. Whilst I met her gaze and she explained to me about my equipment, books and clothes, deep within her eyes I saw the concern she now felt for my welfare and soul, since her questioning from Hecate. I did my best to push these sombre thoughts out of my mind, at least for now. Before lunch, I went and got changed out of my PE kit.

When Raphael saw my enormous bruise, once I had entered the dining hall and sat down next to him, his face became filled with worry.

"God Alex, what happened to your face?" He asked me, leaning over the table and lightly tracing the bruise with his finger, causing me to blush as hundreds of interested eyes turned in my direction.

Swallowing and setting about making myself a melted cheese and tomato sandwich, causing his hand to fall loosely by his side, I explained all in a hushed whisper.

"Let's just say I had a run in with someone in PE who doesn't like me very much." I told him, trying to ignore the fact that my face was now as red as the tomato in my sandwich. "And this was the outcome."

At hearing my answer, Raphael frowned.

Awakening

"Who doesn't like you very much?" He asked me, looking around at the other students in the dining hall with anger written on his face. "Show me who it is and I'll give them a good talking too."
Man. He reminded me so much of David.

In order to fulfil his request, I looked around for Vanessa, but she was nowhere in sight. Then, it struck me that Jasmine wasn't around either.
"They're not here at the moment. However, moving onto more important issues, do you know where Jazz is?" I asked.
Raphael shook his head.
"No." He replied. "I haven't seen her all day. I thought she was with you in PE last lesson, but perhaps I was wrong?" This answer threw me. Nevertheless, I didn't have time to think more about the matter, for Raphael brought up the previous topic of conversation once more. "So...why does this person hate you so much to do that to you?" He asked me, pointing at my bruise. "They must have some serious issues."

After registering his question, I sighed, before telling him about Vanessa and our earlier argument.
"Ouch!" He replied, after listening to my explanation. "Vanessa sounds positively hideous. What's more, to rub even more salt in the wound, you have to share your dorm with her of all people." He frowned. "All in all, I think she should've been named after the devil instead of Lucifer."

I laughed at this comment, before I remembered my Music lesson earlier.
"I think you may be right about Lucifer being an alright, decent guy you know." I swiftly told Raphael, smiling and trying to take my mind off Vanessa. "He seems to be a really nice person, despite his bulky figure."

Raphael grinned back at me.

"I told you so." He laughed, grinning at me and his golden eyes were aglow in amusement. "And, from this discovery, I think that we can all learn the lesson of never judging a book by its cover. What's more," Raphael added, "at least we now know that, despite his name, Lucifer's not a psychopathic demon, who has an intense hatred of the living and is intent on harvesting my soul for all of eternity. Consequently," he concluded, "I think that I can sleep more easily tonight."

I laughed at this comment, now feeling that tingling electricity buzzing inside of me as we locked gazes, his golden eyes holding my ocean ones. Raphael was such a decent, funny and lovely guy and this had been emphasised on more than one occasion since I had initially met him. The way he behaved around me was more or less the same way David had, before my 'awakening'.

His presence felt comfortable and familiar.

Just before I was about to say something else, the bell went, signifying that lunch had ended. After smiling once more, Raphael's eyes searched my own, as I told him I would see him later at dinner. I felt my heart flutter.

Then, I headed off to my Power Control class.

CHAPTER 22: HECATE

As Hecate walked along one of the many long, ancient corridors of the academy, not long after visiting Mrs Frost, she decided that she should probably inform Vladimir about her discoveries. After all, that was one of her duties. Changing direction, she headed towards Vladimir's office, hoping to find him unengaged. As she went to knock on his door, she was presently surprised to hear the headmaster speak in response to her presence, before she had even brushed the old, oak wood with her knuckles.

Clearly, luck was on her side.

"Come in Hecate." He said, his voice low and calm. How he had known she was there when there was no way of seeing or hearing her, for she had always been as silent as mist in her movements, she had no idea. Nevertheless, there were many things that were mysterious about the headmaster so, in the end, although she was curious, she thought it best not to dwell on such matters.

"Vladimir." She replied, nodding politely in his direction, when she had entered his incredible domain. "I just wanted to talk to you about some matters of importance."

The office itself was filled with all sorts of unbelievable objects, some hundreds of years old and filled with ancient history. What's more, either side of the entrance stood two, enormous bookcases brimming with books, some Hecate ached to get her hands on. It was so full of intriguing and unusual devices that Hecate had to slowly shuffle along to get to the headmaster's desk, in case she happened to catch them on her flowing skirt. It was then that she noticed the most interesting item in the whole room, which was situated behind the headmaster. This item wasn't interesting because of its decoration, despite the fact that it was relatively plain apart from the hilt. It wasn't even interesting because of its size for, considering what it was, it was relatively small. No. Instead, it was interesting because it looked so innocent locked in the small, glass cabinet that held it prisoner. Yet, as she drew closer to this mysterious item, Hecate could tell that it was deadly and filled with immense power.

The item that held her attention was, in actual fact, a dagger with a simple outline and beautiful cut. In its hilt, was a small, blood red jewel, which seemed to glitter different colours in the shadowy light of the room.

Vladimir noticed how Hecate was drawn to the dagger in interest.

"I've had this dagger a very long time." He said carefully, making Hecate jump in surprise, as she sat down opposite him. The power and lure of the dagger was enormous.

How had she not noticed it before?

"W...what's it for?" She asked him, trying her best not to keep on looking at it because otherwise, it would ensnare her completely.

In her heart, dark thoughts resided.

"I think you know what its purpose is." Vladimir said simply, highlighting her ominous suspicions. "Therefore, it should never leave this room, unless I say so."

At hearing this disturbing information, Hecate suddenly looked at Vladimir with a worried expression.

"It's powerful." She whispered and, as she spoke these words, she sensed the dagger display this power briefly, in a subtle ripple, affecting the tense atmosphere around the two of them.

Vladimir nodded.

"I know." He replied quietly. Nevertheless, sensing that Hecate had come to him for a different reason entirely, not just because people like her were unconsciously drawn to his office, he asked her why she had visited him.

"Oh." Hecate said, shaking her mind free of the daggers trance. "I bear useful information about the girl whom I spoke to you about earlier - the one I sensed had great power."

At hearing this news, Vladimir rose a little more in his seat and his whole body became alert.

"What is it that you know?" He asked Hecate, his eyes gleaming in interest and voice breathy.

"Well," Hecate began. "I know that her name is Alexandra Raven and that she's blessed with the power to control the element of water."

Vladimir's eyebrows raised at hearing this information, in particular the name of the girl. Hecate noticed his reaction, although she said nothing.

"Really," he replied, "elemental water control? We haven't had someone with that power join this academy since it was built."

Hecate nodded.

At seeing Hecate's reaction, Vladimir was very intrigued. However, he was confused as to why this girl was in the medical wing of all places, after reading Hecate's mind.

"Why's she with Mrs Frost?" He asked Hecate, frowning. "What happened to her?"

Hecate shook her head.

"To be honest, I don't really know," she replied truthfully, "although I think it was something to do with an unfortunate accident in PE. However, regardless of that, I told Mrs Frost to deal with her injuries in the best possible way."

Vladimir nodded in approval. Hecate had done well, extremely well and he told her this with a beaming smile, to which she bowed her head in thanks.

Even so, Vladimir hadn't finished.

"I want you to still check up on this girl – Alexandra Raven. The task in question is far too dangerous for anyone to embark on, let alone those who are of such a young age."

As soon as Vladimir had finished, Hecate nodded in understanding. Subsequently, realising that she should now depart, she hitched up her black, lace skirt, before heading off towards the entrance of Vladimir's office. Before she stepped outside, she remembered that she had another reason for wanting to see Vladimir – a reason that she had kept hidden for the past few days. She had feared that this reason may start a panic or bring bad luck should it ever be spoken aloud. Nevertheless, she knew that she should tell Vladimir, despite her own dread and misgivings.

It was far too important to ignore.

"Vladimir." She said softly. "I've received many messages from the other side recently. The dead are restless and they have told me that Mortimer is in the process of hatching a terrible master plan to ensure his return to Earth. We need to act soon if we wish to stop him."

Vladimir, who had lost himself once more in concerned thoughts, after Hecate had stood up to leave, immediately stiffened. He had felt the darkness around him grow ever colder and menacing over the past month since he had first arranged that initial meeting, to decide what must be done about Mortimer. He had silently prayed his suspicions were incorrect. What a fool he had been to think like that. He now realised, after heeding Hecate's warning. Of course they weren't. He was Vladimir Alcaeus. He was never wrong about matters such as this.

"I understand your concern Hecate." He said slowly, swallowing as his intelligent, blue eyes met hers. "And I've felt this disturbing change myself. However," he continued, "I'll not put anyone in danger, not until I'm completely happy with the decisions being made and we know more about Mortimer's intentions. You know as well as I do that if we are wrong, then Mortimer will destroy those who are put in his way with lethargic ease. Then," he concluded, "once they're gone, he'll turn, eventually, on us."

When Vladimir had finished, Hecate had heard enough. She knew Vladimir's word was final. Therefore, nodding and bidding him goodnight, she exited the room, not once looking back. Even so, this answer did nothing to soothe the foreboding, which was gradually building in her heart.

CHAPTER 23: ALEX

Power Control couldn't have been a more incredible lesson. It was by far the greatest subject ever devised and, to make matters even better, it was taught by the gorgeous young professor who always sat next to Hecate, at the high table, during dinner. As a result of this fact, I was in my element, excuse the pun. In total, there were four of us in this class, three girls and one boy, including me and all of us possessed elemental powers. They, like me, had only just 'awoken' and they came from a variety of backgrounds. As I listened to Mr Allan talk, I realised that he could melt ice with just one look. Mr Allan was a fire bender (rather appropriately) which he demonstrated with rapturous applause by creating a dragon out of thin air and causing it to fly around the training room. It breathed out puffs of smoke through its nose and fire, whilst it soared around our heads. Nevertheless, not long after this breath-taking display, it was our turn to show what we could do, as Mr Allen explained the aims of this starter lesson.

"As it is the first time you have ever undertaken this subject," he explained, wiping his sweaty brow on the back of his hand. His tricks had raised the temperature of the room considerably, although I was pretty sure his presence alone had that effect. "I'll make this first lesson easy. All the same," he continued, "you'll gradually build upon your powers over time, until you eventually become the best that you can possibly be. That is and will always be, our motto and aim."

As Mr Allen spoke, I listened to his words in excited eagerness, which he noted in the small smile he gave me, causing my heart to flutter. There was no doubt that I was going to become one of those silly school girls who fawned over him whenever he was around.

His final words brought me back to reality.

Awakening

"However, before we reach that stage, I'd like to carry out a meet-and-greet session. Therefore, I'd like you to make a small circle on the floor. Then, we can get down to business."

With a curt nod, the four of us sat down. Subsequently, the lesson began. First to speak was a tiny, slim girl with emerald eyes, who smiled shyly at all of us in the group.

"Hi." She began in a small, quiet voice, blushing and fiddling with her flowery top. "My name's Ivy and I can control the element of earth."

Most of us met this introduction with delighted and welcoming smiles, although I rolled my eyes at hearing her name, which would also go on the lengthening list.

When Ivy had finished her introduction, Mr Allen chipped in with a question.

"Would you like to demonstrate your talent Ivy?" He asked her, grinning in such a charming way that her body immediately relaxed and caused me to swoon. "I'm sure that the rest of us would love to see your powers."

After he had finished his request, Ivy's eyes lit up in excitement.

"Sure." She replied smiling before, closing her eyes, she began her demonstration.

Within the room, Mr Allen had set up a variety of objects, which directly linked to our individual elements. As soon as Ivy began using her powers, one of the items in the room abruptly sprung into life. It was a flower pot, full of fertiliser and, as soon as she started her display, the pot started to twitch and wriggle on the table, causing it to vibrate so violently that we all thought it might tip over any second. As I watched in excitement, a single rose was born out of this once solitary container in a beautiful, blood-red colour. This stimulating birth was met with a contented sigh from Ivy, as she realised her demonstration had been a success, before her green eyes gradually opened.

Mr Allen threw her an ecstatic beam.

"Fantastic effort Ivy." He beamed and we all nodded in agreement. "That took a lot of power and effort to create and you showed us that you have a lot of promise."

Ivy threw him a delighted smile, holding his fine-looking gaze for a little longer than was necessary, before he then turned his stare onto the next girl in my class. She was a lot bigger than both Ivy and me, with large stocky arms and legs and dark, grey coloured eyes. What's more, she had a constant scowl plastered on her face and, no matter how hard Mr Allen tried to get her to smile, the glower would not be removed. Whether this was because she was constantly deep in thought, or it was just in her nature to scowl like that, I never knew or asked her for fear of being hit. However, what I did know was that Miss Beast would probably have been her BFFL if they were the same age.

As Miss Beast's doppelganger took centre stage, I soon realised and so did everyone else, that her power was frighteningly impressive. It also duly fit her appearance and nature. This girls name was Gretel and she was an air bender. She demonstrated her power by bending the air around us into eddies of wind. At one terrifying moment, I thought that I was going to be swept away and thrown into a nearby wall. All the same, my heart went out to Ivy, who had gone tremendously pale for fear of her life, as she was so light. Thankfully, Gretel was able to control her powers relatively well and soon, she allowed the air to return to its original state, causing many sighs of relief from the rest of us, including a huge one from Mr Allen. Overall, Mr Allen looked somewhat unnerved by her powerful display, although his extremely windswept hair was positively dreamy.

When we had recovered, Mr Allen praised Gretel quickly, before moving onto the only student in our class who was a boy. The boy was well-built, but not in an unhealthy way and had a glow to his skin. He also had short brown hair and golden eyes, although they weren't as gorgeous as Raphael's.

Mr Allen smiled at him, before asking his name.

"My real name's Samuel." He replied. "However, all my friends here call me Blaze. Also," he added, "I'm half Canadian and a fire bender (he looked at Mr Allen) just like you."

As soon as Blaze had spoken, I noticed that Mr Allen had become extremely eager at hearing this news. I was also delighted to hear that Blaze was half Canadian, for I loved Canada and its wonderful scenery and I thought that his accent was cute (we will keep that to ourselves though).

"Well Blaze." Mr Allen said, after sitting up a little more than before and beaming at him with a glowing smile. "You know the drill, so take it away."

Blaze didn't need telling twice. Settling himself into some form of trance, he focused his attention on the candle, on another nearby table. In an instant, the candle had become a roaring inferno. The moment this happened, I gasped, feeling the heat of the flame scorch my pale skin. The flame he had created was like a hungry beast, ravaging its surroundings and aching to scald anything in its path. As abruptly as the flame had formed, it receded, burning away into nothing. What was left caused a small gasp to be released from my lips, as I was amazed by this boy's obvious control over his volatile power.

He had transformed the candle into a wax bear.

Mr Allen met this demonstration with a vigorous round of applause, which Ivy and I mirrored, for we too were astounded by Blaze's skill (of course Gretel didn't join in). After the applause had died away, I realised that all eyes were now on me.

"Last, but by no means least." Mr Allen said kindly, offering me a reassuring smile. "What's your name and power?"

I felt my nerves take control and I squeaked out an answer.

"A...Alexandra Raven." I stammered, going far redder than Ivy had done. "B...but you can just call me A...Alex and I...I can control the e...element of w...water."

After this declaration, no one spoke, although all looked at me impressed. Even Gretel let slip some of this emotion in her face. After all, for whatever reason it was, water was the penultimate rarest element to be blessed with. Therefore, as all looked at me in admiration, I felt more confident in my powers.

Eventually, Mr Allen spoke.

"Would you like to give us a demonstration?" He asked me, his voice betraying his anticipation at seeing a water bender in action.

I nodded my head in conformation, before I focused on my powers.

Instantly, I felt that familiar tingle of electricity jolt throughout my body. I let myself become consumed with my power. Then, it gradually built until my whole body felt like I was about to explode. Explode I more or less did. My powers burst out of my fingertips like a flood from a dam, making the water in the nearby paddling pool shoot up into the air in numerous, flowing streams. These streams danced about the room, causing everyone to gasp in utter enthrallment and I allowed the water to take on different forms, like animals and shapes before, not just satisfied with that, my powers wanted more. I wasn't ready, nor good enough, to allow that to happen. As a result of this difficulty and my defiance, the sprinklers in the room, just like before with Jessica Wademen, burst into life, causing everyone to shout out in alarm. The instant I heard people's cries of shock, I broke the connection, so that the water collapsed around us, soaking everyone. When I opened my eyes, I didn't know what to expect.

Awakening

Would people be angry with me because I had soaked their clothes?
Would they be amazed at my powers and skill?
Would they hate me forever?
I didn't have to worry about these thoughts, for everyone's stunned faces told me that, despite their drenched clothes, they were in awe of what I could do, even Gretel, which said a lot.
"Wow!" Gretel muttered, looking at me in wonder. "You're super talented."

At seeing her face change so dramatically from a horrific scowl, to complete respect, I burst out laughing.
Soon, everyone else chipped in.
"Yeah she is." Blaze said, grinning at me and giving me a thumbs up.
"She has fantastic skill." Ivy added, causing me to throw her a friendly smile too.
Then, Mr Allen spoke, his good-looking features beaming in delight.
"That has to be the best and most surprising demonstration I've ever had the pleasure of witnessing." He said, clapping his hands together in ecstasy. "However, I think that I need to go away and get out of these clothes." He added. "I, as well as everyone else, am completely sodden after such an inspirational display."
I wouldn't mind helping you out of that top! I thought as he gently tugged at his soaked t-shirt. I saw the same expression in Ivy's face. *After all, I'm sure that I won't be disappointed with what I saw underneath.*

Sadly, Mr Allen didn't give me a chance to live out this fantasy. Instead, we set about mopping up the flooded floor for the remainder of the lesson, laughing and joking amongst each other. Even Gretel joined in, which surprised me immensely. However, this didn't stop the prickle of unease shiver up and down my spine as I left the room. This unease told me that, although I couldn't see them, someone was watching me, observing my behaviour and powers from the shadows.

*

Secretly concealed behind an opaque, two-way mirror, a look of wonder had filled Hecate's face the moment Alexandra had demonstrated her powers. She marvelled at Alexandra's ability and control, for someone who had only just 'awoken' and she also acknowledged the strong level of maturity she presented, despite being young in her years. Maturity was important, especially pitted against the arduous task that lay ahead. It was only after Alexandra had gone, that she dared to reveal her presence.
When she did, her face said everything.

Awakening

CHAPTER 24: ALEX

That evening, whilst we had dinner, I was finally able to solve the mystery disappearance of Jasmine earlier on in the day.

"So...where did you go at lunchtime?" I asked her, frowning in worry as we sat at our usual place in the dining hall. "Raphael and I were concerned about you."

After I had finished, Jasmine clenched her fork a little too tightly, causing the veins in her hand to show significantly. She also flicked her hair over her shoulder furiously, a trait of hers that highlighted her negative state of mind.

"It was that dishonest, two-faced snake's fault." She snarled, now wrathfully stabbing at a roast potato on her plate, as if it were Vanessa's face. "If she hadn't blatantly lied earlier on about not being responsible for hurting you with that netball and using her powers, then we might have avoided detention." Jasmine paused briefly to control her growing temper, before she continued her verbal rant. "Still, because she and I had such a big row, which continued well after Miss Beast had left the gym with you and got me this nail slash on my cheek (she pointed at the long, jagged line down the side of her face) Miss Beast gave us both a lunchtime detention in her office." Jasmine then wrinkled her nose, trying not to gag at the horrible remembrance. "I had to go through a disgustingly smelly pile of gym clothes, which reeked of stale sweat and looked like they hadn't been washed in several years, fearing that I might catch a disease."

As soon as she had finished, I threw her a supportive glance at the sound of this torture. Jasmine acknowledged my look with a grateful smile, before she turned to Raphael and me.

"But enough of my moaning." She eventually sighed. "How was your last lesson?"

Raphael groaned.

"I had Maths for two hours straight." He complained, grumbling. "God, it was awful. Plus, we were looking at algebra – the bane of my life. Seriously, if I see another algebraic equation, I'll knock out my Maths teacher with my mind powers."

Jasmine and I cringed at this news. Neither of us really liked algebra, or Maths for that matter.

"Well...that doesn't sound like fun." Jasmine replied and I nodded in agreement. "I had History, which wasn't too bad I suppose. The most interesting part was learning about our history. Some of the people that came and studied at this academy were very surprising. You know Shakespeare – the genius of a playwright?" Jasmine said, now grinning at the two of us. "He was one of the most famous people to walk these hallways!"

Raphael and I gaped at her in both amazement and disbelief.

"No." I finally retorted, my mouth more or less on the floor. "No way, that's *crazy*."

Jasmine shook her head.

"It's true." She laughed, giggling at our stunned reactions. "He had the power of telepathy. That's how he ended up writing so many incredible works. He read people's minds and invented ideas for his plays and poems from what people were thinking at the time."

At hearing her explanation, I paled considerably. I had always loved and respected Shakespeare ever since I had studded 'A Midsummer Night's Dream' in Year Seven.

"But that would make him a thief, not a genius." I replied. "He basically stole other people's ideas."

Jasmine roared with laughter at this comment, which was nice to hear after her previous annoyance.

"Yeah." She grinned. "I never thought about it that way, but I suppose he did. Still," she continued, "he became the only richest, revered and undiscovered "thief" ever to make a successful living, so you can't really complain. He was practically a celebrity! Also," she added in a cynical tone. "You can't argue against the fact that there're still people today who take ideas from other people and spin them into their own work."

I met Jasmine's last comment with silence and, for the rest of the time, my thoughts were constantly consumed with what Jasmine had told me about Shakespeare. Even when I went to bed, I still thought of this issue.

Eventually, I managed to fall asleep.

It was around three in the morning when the horrific nightmare began. The nightmares started when I dreamt that I was in an urban, built-up area, hurrying along a filthy pathway in my high heeled shoes and gazing occasionally at the starlight sky above me. I constantly glanced over my shoulder, feeling that I was being followed and fear filled my heart. As I ran, the moon leered down at my quivering form from above, its harsh silver rays sending shivers of unease shooting around my body, rather than offering me comfort. Suddenly, I stumbled on an empty, glass bottle, narrowly avoiding falling heavily onto the grimy pavement. Then, my fears crashed down upon me like an avalanche. The moment I fell, I was hit from behind by a powerful force. I cried out in pain, as I was roughly pulled into a side alley by my arm, so hard in fact that I thought my shoulder had been dislocated.

Subsequently, I had a gun waved frantically in my face.

"Do as you're told and you won't get hurt." My attacker spat in a deep, gruff voice, before he clicked off the safety trigger on the gun, so I knew he meant business.

"W...what do you want from me?" I stammered except I realised that bizarrely, it wasn't my voice at all. Instead, this voice was higher in pitch and not as soft. "T...take my bag if that's what you want, just don't hurt me."

I was crying now, or whoever I was supposed to be was crying. Thick, hot tears fell from my salty eyelashes, staining my satin, purple dress. I saw my attacker smile, his lips peeling back to reveal rotting teeth.

"Now, now." He said mockingly. "We don't need any tears. As long as you cooperate, all will be fine."

In a blinding, gigantic black ball of energy, two hideous, terrifying and otherworldly creatures formed out of nowhere, causing both my attacker and I to scream in horror, panic and shock. I felt a lump form in my throat.

"What the —" My attacker went to swear, dropping the gun in astonishment. He was interrupted by one of the creatures, whose entire body was on fire and stunk of burning flesh, causing the two of us to gag.

As I frantically tried to cover my nose, I cowered in terror and disbelief.

"Are you Josssseph Cunningssss?" This creature hissed, its black eyes, or what could only be considered to be eyes, for they were more like gaping holes, flashing.

After hearing this question, my assailant could not form any words. Instead, as he paled considerably, his mouth moved up and down like a guppy.

"Ssssspeak earthly mortal!" The second creature abruptly cried, which was smaller than the first but shook constantly, its body appearing pale and weak. "I demand that you ansssswer ussssss."

Unfortunately for my attacker and me, this unearthly being also gave off the repulsive odour of decay. Although my attacker struggled against the pull both terrifying creatures had over him,

Awakening

after hearing this forceful command, he rapidly found himself speaking, his voice quivering.

"Y...yes." He told them, cowering. "Yes, that's my n...name."

As soon as my assailant had correctly identified himself, I saw how both creatures smiled maliciously at each other, pleased that they had found the right person. It was then that Joseph burst into a fit of talking, now pleading for his life.

"A...are you demons?" He cried, now sobbing profusely. He looked pitiful. "If you are, then p...please don't h...hurt me?"

Funny how the tables had now turned.

After hearing this plea, both creatures unexpectedly burst into terrible laughter. This cackling caused a major power cut throughout the city and glass rained down upon us from a nearby street lamp, which had exploded, causing me to scream. Then, in a flash with a flick of his fiery hand, black, snake-like chains began to encircle Joseph's arms and legs, causing him to shout out in pain and alarm, before the fiery creature spoke.

"Of courssssse we're demonssss imbecile." He hissed. "I mean look at usssss. Do we look like kindly ssspiritssss?" The creature laughed again before continuing. "Assss for not hurting you, that issss out of the quessssstion."

As if to emphasise this fact, he tugged hard on the fiery chains, causing Joseph to shriek in agony, as what felt like a thousand knives struck him at once. These chains succeeded in wrapping around his body and causing the repulsive demon to smirk, delighted by the pain he was inflicting. The moment Joseph was fully trapped, the demon turned to his companion.

"Time to go." He said, grinning cruelly. "Our massssster isss expecting ussss."

Just as the two creatures were about to step once more into the swirling black vortex with their terrified prey in tow, one of the demons - the one who constantly shook, saw me shivering by a collection of bins.

"What about her?" He asked the other, pointing at my shaking form.

"Sssshe hasss witnessssed our work."

Immediately, the fiery demon turned to face me, his black holes boring into mine.

"We kill her!" He replied casually, as if it was part of his job description. What's more, as if to emphasise his command, I felt as if my entire body was slowly being torn apart, causing me to scream like I had never screamed before.

Then, my whole world went black.

CHAPTER 25: ALEX

I woke up, screaming until my throat was raw, despite the fact that the nightmare had ended. Sweat covered my skin like a fiery blanket and I shivered like a leaf. Nevertheless, the worst part of the whole situation was the fact that I could still smelt the repulsive aroma of burnt and rotten flesh that had clung to the forms of both horrifying creatures. This implied that my nightmare might not have been a nightmare at all. Instead, in actual fact, it felt as if it had been very real indeed.
I shivered with shock, fear and unease.

Jasmine was up in an instant, as soon as she heard my terrified shrieks and came hurrying to stand by the side of my bed.
"Alex." She cried, eyes wild with fear. "What's the matter? What's wrong?"

Slowly, I inhaled deep breaths, gradually feeling my heart rate slow down. I turned to face her, tears forming in the corner of my eyes.
"Oh Jazz." I whispered, thankful that I was here in this room and not in that filthy alleyway, dying. "I've just had the most terrifying nightmare. It felt s...so...real!"

Jasmine threw her arms comfortingly around me and stroked my hair.
"It's OK Alex." She muttered quietly, allowing me to weep into her shoulder. "It was only a nightmare – nothing more. Would you like me to get you a drink?"

I nodded, muttering that I would be grateful for a drink of water, for my throat felt like sandpaper. As I heard her bustling about in the bathroom, deep down, despite her reassurance, I knew that she was wrong. It wasn't just a nightmare. I realised, quivering in terror. No.

Instead, I was 99.9% positive that what I had just experienced was, as absurd as it sounded, a vision!

*

Hecate felt the presence of death within the walls of the academy, as soon as the clock had struck midnight. Waking instantly and hastily getting to her feet, she pulled on her black, silk dressing gown. Subsequently, she quietly closed the door behind her and set about hurrying along the corridors in the darkness, her long, lacy gown flapping frantically about her knees. To be honest, because of her powers, she felt more at home when it was dark. Although it sounded strange, she thought that she could almost see better during the night than when it was daylight. She followed the scent of death like a dog might smell out a bone. Unfortunately, although unsurprisingly, the stench of death led her to the dormitory where she knew Alexandra resided. This knowledge once again emphasised her suspicions about the girl's fate.

When the smell of death intensified, Hecate realised she needed to explore the situation further. As quiet as a mouse, she slipped into the dorm area, before coming to stand directly outside Alexandra's room.

It reeked of pulsating evil.

Closing her icy blue eyes, Hecate's beautiful face fell into a trance. She psychically felt out Alexandra's presence. Her heart stopped when she realised what Alexandra was experiencing. To begin with, Alexandra was having a nightmare. That much was obvious. However, Hecate knew that it was most definitely not a normal nightmare. Instead, somehow, as she had been dreaming, she had become drawn to another living person, a female, who lived far away from here in some bustling, grimy city.

Eventually, she had become 'psychically attached' to her soul.

Hecate didn't know why this had happened. She was astounded that such a young person would be capable of achieving such powerful connections. After all, she only knew of a small handful of people who were able to psychically link to others, including herself and Vladimir Alcaeus. Nonetheless, she knew that Alexandra was different. Shaking, she tried to put these troublesome thoughts out of her mind for now, ensuring that she currently focused all her attention on experiencing the vision alongside Alexandra. As she saw the events Alexandra was witnessing unfold, she realised why this strange occurrence was happening.

As soon as Hecate saw Mortimer's servants appear and watched their sinister actions unfold, she put two and two together, finally concluding that Alexandra was indeed having a psychic vision. She also concluded that, because of all the events and feelings she had witnessed and felt so far, she must be linked to Mortimer and his dealings somehow. After all, it couldn't be a coincidence that she had psychically attached herself to a girl who was witnessing dealings with Mortimer, in addition to Alexandra demonstrating unbelievable powers within her first lesson earlier on in the day...could it?

As the psychic link ended abruptly and Hecate was relieved to hear Alexandra being comforted by her friend, she became troubled by what she had just witnessed. Mortimer's servants were clearly finding mortal humans who fitted a certain criterion. Perhaps it involved those who were the evilest of their kind? After all, that made perfect sense, considering that they had taken a criminal of wicked intentions and history to their master. Mortimer himself was as wicked as you could possibly get and then some. All the same, as Hecate hypothesised, she suddenly panicked. Why was something deep inside her telling her that she was wrong in her suspicions and it wasn't to do with how evil someone was? Instead, it was to do with another reason entirely.

All in all, this was very grave news indeed.

Doing her best to collect her swirling thoughts, Hecate leaned against the door, breathing heavily. Ultimately, when she had somewhat composed herself, she muttered a protective prayer, before walking slowly back to her own room. As she did so, all the while, she was consumed by dark torments.

CHAPTER 26: ALEX

Since that nightmarish episode, the weeks seemed to fly by. Over the course of this time, Raphael and I seemed to bond more, particularly over the topic of superheroes. What's more, I started to talk more to Lucifer, after we got paired together in Music for a practical task. I came to realise that there was more to him than met the eye. Before long, I realised that I hadn't written an e-mail to my parents — something that I had promised to do. Therefore, after waking up early and thinking about what I could say, I eventually managed to type my thoughts.

My e-mail went as follows:

From: Alex4chocolate@btinternet.com
To: Cathy&Toby@btinternet.com
Date: 27th October 2015
Time: 7:30 am
Subject: Hi at long last from Vladimir's academy.

Dear Mum and Dad,

I can't tell you how much I'm enjoying being at Vladimir's academy. There is only one word I can use to sum up what it is like living here — AMAZING. That includes the academy itself, which is so ancient and gothic that it puts 'Mad Al's House', with all his ghosts and ghouls, to shame. Sometimes I feel that I'm still living in the dark ages. I mean, Vladimir still uses candles instead of normal lighting for crying out loud. Therefore, as you can probably understand, I was shocked when I found out that this place had Wi-Fi!

As for the grounds, which surround the academy, they're HUGE. I love exploring this area although, at the moment, because it is October, they're literally swimming in mud. This is very annoying,

Adele Rose

particularly because, when I first arrived here, my scout wasn't debriefed about the change in meeting location. Therefore, we both ended up taking a mud bath on our way up to the academy. Still, despite this misfortune, there's a gigantic lake, which students can explore after hiring a range of boats, in addition to a small, mysterious island in the middle of this vast expanse of water. Also, in the academy itself, there's a library, which I've yet to explore but am excited to use. I'm especially eager to visit the library because I've been given permission to do some ancestry digging on great grandfather Alistair.

Most of the teachers I've met so far are lovely as well, both in personality and in teaching. My favourite professors include my Music teacher – Miss Crotchet (I know, cool right?) who looks like a real-life version of the Disney princess 'Snow White'. She also has the greatest respect for great grandfather - Alistair and is the one who is kindly letting me research more about our family history. Then, there's Mr Allen, who's my Power Control Teacher and is a fire bender. He is extremely handsome - the eye candy of the school for want of a better phrase and is tremendously talented. I also respect him because of his passion, drive and ability to see the good in people, even if they can't see this themselves. All in all, I think that it's a shame he's too old for me, plus being my teacher.
Even so, we can all dream...right?

With regards to Vladimir Alcaeus, he's as incredible as people describe, although I've not had the pleasure of talking to him personally. He exuberates power and authority and I'm not sure if I'd want to get on his bad side. I reckon he'd pack a punch or two, even if he's getting on. There are those here though, teachers and students alike, who are on my 'not hot' list. In terms of teachers, there's one teacher, called Miss Beast, who couldn't fit this description better in personality and appearance.

Awakening

Furthermore, her job is ironically, wait for it...PE.

Miss Beast has the character and appearance of an ox on heat and she enjoys ripping people apart verbally, as well as physically, I think, if she ever got the chance. She takes great pleasure in emphasising her authority over others and, as you can imagine, therefore, has no friends or admirers whatsoever. Another teacher I'm not so keen on is Hecate. She's one of the more mysterious professors at the academy and is deputy headmistress. Hecate dresses in all black, is extremely pale, unearthly beautiful and has the most chilling eyes I've ever known. All in all, she comes across as one of 'The Walking Dead' – except alive and far prettier. The main reason why I'm not so keen on her includes the fact that she seems to be a stalker. It's as if she's constantly around wherever I go and all because I happened to meet her gaze during dinner on the first night at the academy, resulting in us sharing a weird "connection". I mean, as I'm writing this e-mail, the whole thing sounds like a horror movie script and even writing about her is giving me the chills. Nonetheless, the worst person out of them all has to be Vanessa.

Vanessa is your classic rich, spoilt, rude, heartless and superior snob. I could go on with similar adjectives to describe her, but I'd probably end up making this e-mail a thousand pages long. Vanessa is so awful that she even had the nerve to tell me, after I asked her why she disliked me so much, that it is because I'm ugly, that I've got no fashion sense whatsoever and that my background is shameful. After delivering these pathetic allegations, I told her that she needed psychiatric help, which didn't go down too well. I ended up with a bruised face thanks to the ball that she wacked in my direction during netball but, don't worry, the bruise is already going down. All the same, I can hear Jasmine (my best friend here, who can control the weather) calling me because we need to go down to breakfast. Therefore, I send you lots of love with this e-mail and can you also *send my love to my brother and David. I hope that they, in addition to you, are doing well.*

All my love,
Alex xxxxx

When I had finished writing my e-mail, after acknowledging Jasmine's calls for me to leave, I pressed 'send' and hoped that my parents would reply as soon as possible. Then, Jasmine and I set off in the direction of the dining hall, our stomach's rumbling appreciatively.

CHAPTER 27: ALEX

After a wholesome breakfast, I left early to collect my books for my first lesson. Just as I turned around to leave for Music, Vanessa's spiteful face met mine, as I came to the bottom of the dormitory stairs.

"Well girls, look at who we've just bumped into on our way to first period?" Vanessa grinned nastily at me, flashing a smile at the small huddle of cronies who had gathered around her, including her BF Tiffany and I realised that, up until now, I had steadily been avoiding her, even in the lessons we shared. "Why, it's the screaming banshee."

At hearing this vindictive comment, all of her followers burst out laughing in hideous cackles, ironically sounding more like banshees than I had during that nightmarish experience, which thankfully hadn't repeated since. I blushed red. Clearly, Vanessa must have heard me screaming and shouting, during that time and now that she had me cornered and vulnerable, she wanted to torment me about it.

Scowling, I glared back at her, shaking in anger.

"Ha-ha, very funny." I said sarcastically, not holding back. "Although it won't be as funny as it will be when my fist meets your eye."

A gasp from her companions met this retort and all began to whisper amongst themselves, shocked by my spunk. Even I was surprised by my guts to say such a violent answer. So far, my reaction to Vanessa's jibes hadn't been nearly so volatile. However, Vanessa wasn't about to lose the argument, or be humiliated. Plus, she didn't think I had it in me to fight back physically.

"Yeah right." She rolled her eyes. "As if you would have the backbone to pull off a move like that, let alone even know where my eyes are in my face."

Again, this was met with a delighted roar of approval from her friends and she grinned like she had already won the battle. As a result of this reaction, her nerve to say such a condescending and unpleasant comment and, due to her violent behaviour in Netball, I made her eat her words.

A darkness rose within me.

Quicker than lightening, she was on the floor, her golden hair sprawled about her head like a halo. Moaning in agony, she clutched her right eye. As soon as this incident had happened, Vanessa's friends hurriedly crowded around her, offering words of support and trying to help her to her feet. These actions were met with numerous curses, mostly aimed at me. I, on the other hand, felt on fire, as adrenaline charged around my body. I watched her writhe about on the floor, her beautiful, designer dress becoming dirty and crinkled, although my wrist hurt a little due to the force at which I had hit Vanessa.

I had hit Vanessa.

Oh my god! I couldn't believe I had just hit another person, let alone Vanessa of all people, despite the fact that I had been itching to spoil that perfect face ever since arriving at the academy. I hadn't even hit Jessica Wademen and she was up there on my 'hit' list.

As I stood there watching Vanessa shakily get to her feet, her right eye rapidly matching the same colour as her dress, I began to grin. It was a shame that Jasmine hadn't been around to see my sharp moves.

"Touché." I said, pointing at her growing bruise, which caused her to wince. "Now we're even on the injury front."

If looks could kill, I would've been dead by now. Vanessa glared at me with a profuse amount of venom. However, much to my surprise, deep within her eyes, I saw another emotion – fear.

Vanessa was afraid of...of...me.

"You'll regret doing that!" Vanessa hissed through gritted teeth, blinking back her tears. Then, with a snarl of rage, trying to keep a hold of what pride she had left, she flung off her fawning followers and charged off down the hall, towards first period.

When she was gone, I burst into laughter, unable to contain my shock and delight at my behaviour. From not being able to defend myself barely a week ago, I had turned into a person who could actually have the bravado to punch someone. What's more, the person who I had punched had showed signs of being frightened of me. It was insane. Bubbling with adrenaline, I set off excitedly to tell Jasmine what I had done, shock still flowing through my veins.

CHAPTER 28: ALEX

"You did what?" Jasmine replied, her mouth agape after I had told her about hitting Vanessa, although she looked significantly impressed.

"I know right." I retorted, still bubbling with adrenaline. "I still can't believe I actually punched Vanessa and wiped that snooty smile off her face."

Jasmine threw me a delighted smile.

"Girl...I'm so proud of you." She said, throwing her arm around me. "You're undeniably living up to the badass quality of your name."

I laughed, pleased that her thoughts matched my own. Nevertheless, Miss Crotchet, who had been lenient in letting us talk in Music so far, had had enough.

"Girls!" She said sharply, raising her eyebrows. "Unless you're talking about your composition, which I doubt very much, you need to stop your current topic of conversation, however exciting it may be and focus on your work."

As soon as she had reprimanded us, Jasmine and I apologised abruptly for disrupting the lesson. Both of us liked Miss Crotchet a great deal. Therefore, we did as she had instructed us to do. Even so, we both knew that this conversation was far from over. The moment the bell went for second period, Miss Crotchet came over to us and gave me the permission slip she had promised.

"Thanks." I smiled up at her, after she had finished. "And we're both very sorry for disrupting your lesson."

Jasmine nodded her head in agreement, but Miss Crotchet just waved us off.

"I accepted your apology earlier." She replied. "All the same, just remember to keep gossip outside my classroom in the future and enjoy reading that file."

Awakening

Once more, I thanked her again for the permission slip, before Jasmine and I headed off towards English together.

The two of us resumed our conversation.

"So...how hard did you hit her?" Jasmine asked me, eager for the full low-down, as we walked along the corridor.

"Pretty hard." I replied, smiling. "She'll have a huge bruise like I did over her right eye by now I reckon."

"I wonder if she'll go to the medical ward," Jasmine added, "if it's that bad?"

I shook my head.

"I doubt that very much." I answered. "She'd rather suffer than give me the satisfaction of degrading her ego even more than I already have by visiting such a place."

Jasmine nodded.

"I suppose you're right." She finished up by saying. "Still, I can't wait to see your handiwork."

As it happened, Jasmine didn't have to wait for long to see Vanessa's mammoth bruise, for she was actually in our English class. When Vanessa saw me sitting at the back of the classroom, she threw me a heated glare, which looked funny as her right eye was beginning to close up, before she sat in a seat over the other side of the room, sulking.

Jasmine nudged me.

"Blimey. I didn't think you'd hit her that hard!" She gawked at Vanessa, along with others in the room, causing her to go bright red. "You really gave her a right hander there."

The instant Jasmine had finished talking, I threw her a grin. However, to be honest, when I saw how much Vanessa was being subjected to whispered mutterings, gaping and giggles, I suddenly felt awful. Sure, she had been really unkind to me since we had first met. Sure, she had called me unpleasant names. Sure, she had hit me with the netball. All the same, knowing how much the comments going around stung, as I had been there, done it and got the t-shirt, I felt extremely guilty. This guiltiness was further heightened when our teacher dismissed Vanessa early because, despite her protests, he was not happy with how bad her bruise was rapidly becoming. Thankfully, her pride meant that she refused to tell him how she had gotten the bruise in the first place. Still, as she spoke, I lay back further in my seat, wanting the ground to swallow me up.

Shame flooded my heart.

Awakening

CHAPTER 29: ALEX

Although I did my best to distract myself from these upsetting thoughts throughout the remainder of the lesson and the rest of the day, my guilt and awkwardness proved to be difficult to hide. Rumours surrounding Vanessa's bruise swept around the academy like wildfire, much like they had done when I had been hurt in netball. To make matters worse, after Raphael had heard about me punching Vanessa, he seemed to be the only one, apart from Vanessa's followers, who was unimpressed by this action. Instead, his face darkened significantly and he looked at me strangely, as if to say: "I never thought that you would stoop to her level." This reaction stung like crazy, ever since my emotions for him had gradually been strengthening the longer we were in each other's company. Nevertheless, the exciting news at dinner, delivered by Vladimir, seemed to ease the tension temporarily.

"So...now that my talk about end of term assessments is over." Vladimir continued, clapping his hands together eagerly and making those who had drifted off in sleepiness jump to attention. "I'd like to talk to you about the Halloween Ball, as it's almost October 31st."

As soon as he had uttered the last word, the room exploded in a buzz of eagerness. This Halloween Ball sounded exciting. Therefore, everyone abruptly turned to listen to the headmaster, in a babble of anticipation. At seeing everyone's excitement, Vladimir chuckled in delight, before he relieved all who were present of their anticipation. "Every 31st October," Vladimir began, "we have a Halloween Ball. It's a traditional celebration, which has predominately seen much laughter, excitement and merriment throughout the years. Therefore, this tradition will continue on that very date, in much of the same fashion." Vladimir paused for a moment, to allow the whispered mutterings of excitement to resume once more, before he continued his explanation. This was greeted with a hushed silence. "This dining hall will be host location for that particular evening and your afternoon lessons will be cancelled so that we, as teachers, can organise and decorate the room. Furthermore," Vladimir added, "there are two requirements. All of you, including the staff here at this academy, are to dress up for the occasion and, if you can, find a date (that word sounded so unnatural on Vladimir's tongue. Consequently, it caused a few nervous and amused giggles from various students) for this long-established event." Vladimir rounded up his speech. "And so, with that being said, let's begin eating because, I don't know about you, but I'm feeling very hungry indeed."

As soon as the food had been put on the table and everyone began to eat, Jasmine turned to Raphael and me in exhilaration.
"Oooo...a Halloween Ball." She gushed. "It sounds like so much fun."
"If you say so." Raphael replied, his voice grumpy.

Fearfully, I put this down to the whole "Vanessa incident".
After hearing his moody tone, Jasmine turned to him, stung.
"Oh, lighten up." She quipped. "Halloween only happens once a year."

Realising that Raphael wasn't interested, she turned to me, her eyes sparkling.
"I already know what I'm going as." She replied, trying to distract herself. "I can create a really cute cat costume from the clothes in my bedroom. What about you?"
I shook my head, not really in the mood for discussing the topic, particularly because Raphael seemed so irritable.
"I don't really know to be honest." I replied. "I'll see what I can do closer to the time."

Jasmine looked at me surprised by my lack of enthusiasm.

Awakening

"Oh, why are the two of you such spoil sports?" She cried. "It's only a Halloween Ball for crying out loud." Nevertheless, even this cry of protest did nothing to change the darkening atmosphere. With a sigh of frustration and a glower, Jasmine turned to the student next to her and began talking excitedly to her instead, leaving Raphael and I to dwell on regretful and gloomy thoughts for the remainder of the evening.

CHAPTER 30: ALEX

After dinner, everyone else, apart from our small trio, seemed to go to bed on a high. Feeling tense, I tried to lighten the atmosphere by smiling more as I said goodbye to Raphael. He nodded a reply in my direction. However, after that simple acknowledgement, he then headed towards his dormitory, not once looking back.

"I wonder what's got his pants in a twist?" Jasmine said moodily after we watched him go, before the two of us finished walking up the remainder of stairs and entered our room. "He's been so grouchy all evening for no apparent reason." I shrugged, as I threw myself onto my bed, although I knew very well why he was being so grumpy. "It's so annoying because I really hoped that he would asked me to be his date for the Halloween Ball." She continued on, oblivious to my stiffening body. "Now though, he seems so disinterested in the whole thing that I think I might skip it altogether, which sucks for people like me who love this time of year."

I made no reply to answer her for immediately, as soon as she had finished, I felt the green-eyed monster rear its head in significant jealousy. I tried to push it down and, during this process, I hid my face in my wardrobe, as I searched for some clean pajamas. Nevertheless, I could feel Jasmine's intense stare on the back of my neck. Therefore, I forced myself to grumble a response, trying to keep my voice as calm and steady as possible.

"Yeah, well, he's probably just really tired, that's all." I answered lamely and she looked at me as if I had burst her bubble.

So much for being a supportive friend. I thought, wincing slightly. *Particularly after all she did to help you when you had that nightmarish vision.*

However, a dark voice added, *when that friend has eyes for the guy you want, you're not exactly going to offer the best advice are you?*

Suddenly, Jasmine looked at me strangely, as if she was able to read my current train of thought. All the same, shaking her head and sighing, she went into the bathroom to get ready for bed, closing the bathroom door a little too harshly for my liking. Doing my best to ignore her, I curled up into a tight ball.

God, I've been such a flipping idiot. I mentally cried. *So much for me thinking that I was being 'oh so clever' and 'impressive' for actually hitting Vanessa. Instead, I feel positively guilty and the guy who I'm beginning to like is now giving me the cold shoulder.*
I currently SUCK!

Groaning, I rolled over and begun to punch my pillow violently. I had screwed up badly. I realised, as I hit the soft fabric with intent. Really, really badly. As I collapsed onto my back, exhausted, I realised that I had to find a way to make things up with Raphael and I hoped that he would be willing to forgive me for what I had done.

CHAPTER 31: ALEX

I decided to take the necessary action after I met Raphael at breakfast the following morning. All night I had been plagued with unpleasant dreams. Therefore, concluding that I needed to sort things out fast, I spoke to him in quick succession, after Jasmine had left us in order to talk to one of her fellow History students.

"Raphael." I asked him cautiously. "Can I speak to you for a moment?"

Raphael suddenly looked at me concerned, as he heard the anxiety in my voice. Due to this emotion, I relaxed slightly. Perhaps he was already forgiving me and his coldness towards me yesterday was just a fleeting reaction?

I hoped so.

"Of course you can." He told me. "What is it that you want to say?"

Hastily scanning the area and seeing Jasmine firmly occupied, I hinted at the dining room door.

"Is it OK if we talk somewhere more private?" I asked him. "I feel as if this room has ears."

His eyebrows rose at hearing my request.

Nevertheless, he was only too happy to comply.

"Sure." He answered and soon, the two of us were walking through the long corridors in silence, before we were outside the academy and heading in the direction of the great lake.

When we had put a satisfying distance between us and any prying ears, I spoke in a stream of confused thoughts.

"Your mood yesterday changed after you heard about me hitting Vanessa." I began, blushing all the while I spoke. "Did you not think that that was the right thing to do? After all, she's been unnecessarily mean to me since I arrived."

After I had asked him my question, he looked at me, surprised that I had managed to suss him out so well. Eventually, sighing, he ran a frustrated hand through his dark hair.

"To be honest Alex." He replied, his golden eyes flashing with conflicting emotions. "When I heard about your fight, I was proud of you for sticking up for yourself. That's an admirable quality, in any person. However," he concluded, "I don't think that you should've lashed out like that. You were basically stooping yourself to her level and I didn't like to hear that you'd done that. That's not you, or what you stand for!"

I nodded my head, confirming that my suspicions were correct.

"I'm sorry if I upset you." I responded, my voice now small. "I didn't mean to hurt you."

He threw me a small smile.

"It's alright." He answered, his golden eyes now meeting mine. "But it's really Vanessa whom you need to apologise to, not me."

As soon as he had spoken, I knew that he was absolutely right. Even so, I just didn't know how I could possibly forgive the girl who had made my life hell since arriving here, for unjust reasons. In the end, I nodded to prove that I understood where he was coming from and he smiled, pleased that I could see his intentions. The silence lengthened between the two of us for a brief moment, before Raphael asked me a question, which caused my heart to stop.

"Alex." He asked me, his voice now timid and it was his turn to blush. "You know Vladimir told us about the Halloween Ball yesterday and about the two requirements?"

I nodded, although inside, I was a jumble of emotions and thoughts.

"Well...I was wondering if you would like to be my...well...my date for the evening?"

I couldn't breathe. It was as if the whole world had stopped turning.

"Raphael I...I..." I couldn't speak.

The majority of my body was screaming YES!

It was then that I remembered Jasmine and her comment last night that she hoped Raphael would ask her to the Halloween Ball. She had looked so hopeful. I went the colour of beetroot, as I saw Raphael's expectant, yearning face. Before long, I felt the words he desperately wanted to hear form on the tip of my tongue. Nonetheless, I realised that I couldn't betray Jasmine like this, not after what she had done for me since arriving at the academy.

At the last second, I revealed all to him about Jasmine's confession.

"Oh Raphael, I'd love you to take me to the Ball." I told him passionately. "But Jasmine's so hoping that you would ask her to this event. She really, really wants to go with you," I finalised, "especially as you mean a lot to her, although she's far too shy to tell you this directly."

At hearing my rejection, Raphael's features abruptly fell and his eyes swam with hurt. I could tell that I had disappointed him considerably with my answer. Nevertheless, after I had given him my reasons for turning him down, deep within his eyes, although they were sad, he recognized my fierce loyalty.

He gave me a brief, sharp nod.

"You're such a faithful friend." He eventually replied, after another pause. "Jasmine's very lucky to have you by her side." Then, turning his back on me, his shoulders slumped in deflation, he headed back towards the academy.

For a few moments, after he had gone, my mind went crazy. *Why?* It screamed at me. *Why did you let him go? He was desperate to take you to the Halloween Ball. You saw it in his eyes.*

As I listened to my brain, my body yearned to run after Raphael – to take everything back and to tell him how I really felt. It took so much effort to stay there, not moving. After a short while, I realised that, at that moment in time, I had done the right thing. Raphael may have meant a lot to me but so did Jasmine, especially after all she had done to help me. Subsequently, it was my turn to leave the lake and, as I had free periods all morning, I decided that now was the time to visit the library. I hoped that my quest would take my mind off my distressed heart.

CHAPTER 32: ALEX

The library could be summed up in three words – enormous, ancient and dusty – extremely dusty. It was exactly like those magnificent libraries you more or less see in every gothic movie. What's more, I was thankful that I was not an asthmatic, for this was most definitely their form of hell. Ultimately, because the library was so gigantic, I decided that I would ask the librarian, who was currently making books zoom about the room with her mind, where I needed to go to access the files I wanted. She met my gaze with her wizened features, once she had finished placing the last book in the right place.

"Yes." She croaked. "What can I do for you?"

I showed her my permission slip.

"I'm looking for the area that deals with these files." I told her. "I've got permission to access one of them."

She threw me a haughty look.

"I can see that." She said, looking miffed and harshly prodding the piece of paper in my hand. "I'm not blind yet." Nevertheless, despite her peeved state, she pointed a wrinkled finger at the far end of the enormous room, to where a roped fence cut the library into one of its numerous sections. "The area you're looking for is past that rope," she added, stamping the form. "But make sure you put the files back where you found them once you're finished. I'm fed up of finding Bronte next to Wordsworth and Dickens next to Shakespeare."

Trying to stifle a smile and hide my shock, I nodded in understanding, before I made my way towards the area, which she had kindly highlighted to me. Then, ducking under the roped fence, I made my way through the numerous alphabet-marked shelves, until I found the one I wanted. My great grandfather was thankfully

Awakening

located in the right place, under the letter of 'S' for 'Silverstone' and I pulled out his file in interest and excitement. Subsequently, I brought it over to a nearby table, where I flicked on the old lamp, plonked my behind on a dusty chair and set about reading its contents.

What I found inside was fascinating.

Alastair Silverstone's file included a detailed account of his life, from his birth in 1892 and his 'awakening' in 1908, right up until his death in 1966. I realised when reading this that this meant that the early years of his life occurred during the Victorian Era. Therefore, that was, in my opinion, pretty cool. This ancestry file began with a detailed account of where he lived when he was born, which was in the English countryside, not far from London. It also discussed how my great grandfather became fascinated by the publication of Darwin's 'On the Origin of Species' (1859) when he turned fifteen and in the subject of Science. Consequently, I realised, it was no great surprise really that, a year later, he was blessed with the gift of being able to communicate with animals.

I re-read the story of his 'awakening' in high amusement, for it was indeed a funny tale. This gem was located in a short interview, which was situated in the back of his file. The interview was conducted by a scouting and counselling team, who had been called in to support my great grandfather's mother (Maria Silverstone) and to transcribe exactly what had happened that day.

The interview went as follows:

Date: 17th April 1908
Time: 10:34am
Location: The home of Alistair Silverstone and his parents
Interviewer: William Dent
Interviewee: Maria Silverstone

[Interview Commenced]

WD: "Please can you describe to me your initial reaction when you saw your son talking to your finest cow, known to all as 'Old Bessie'?"

MS: "Utter shock, worry and disbelief – so much so that I thought I was having a heart attack. When I first saw him talking to 'Old Bessie', I initially thought that my son had been kicked in the head by her, resulting in severe, mental delusions. However, when I saw that there was no trace of a fractured skull, bleeding on the ground or in his ginger hair, I didn't know what to think. It was only after my husband came rushing out of the house, to see what all my shouting was about, that he realised what had happened and frantically tried to inform me about the fact that our son had 'awoken' – something that should have happened well before we even got married."

WD: "Is it true that you threatened to murder your husband for keeping his 'awakening' heritage a secret?"

MS: [Shouting] "It bloody well is true. I wanted to murder him ten times over for his deceitful lies and I decided that I'd use his favourite shotgun to commit the deadly deed. Still, after many promises of lavish presents, romantic evenings and bottles of gin, I eventually accepted the truth, although I still feel I need counselling!"

WD: "Of course you're entitled to counselling. We've a specialist team waiting to help you outside."

MS: "Thank you. You seem very nice people, despite your...talents."

WD: "You're welcome." [Looks somewhat offended by the last comment. Nevertheless, after a moment of awkward silence, the questions continue].

WD: "Let's talk about your son now. Where's he going?"

Awakening

[Alistair Silverstone had just disappeared around the back of the family house]

MS: "Oh, he probably went off to talk to the chickens now, as well as Burt, the potbellied pig. He seemed eager this morning to know their thoughts on the matter of farming, as well as their opinions on being slaughtered for their meat. [Looking extremely surprised] Did you know he told me earlier that he wanted to be something called a 'vegetarian'? I guess that what the animals have told him over the past few days, since he 'awakened', has changed his mind about the meat industry. [She suddenly chuckles, before rolling her eyes]. I wouldn't be surprised if he gets us chomping on rabbit food as well soon."

WD: "He sounds a charming and lovely boy, who clearly has a strong affinity for animals."

MS: "Oh yes, he's always loved animals and living on the farm, surrounded by nature."

WD: "So...because of this fierce love of animals, what do you think Alistair will end up doing in the near future?"

MS: "Oh, he's always been a very bright boy you know? I don't know where he gets his brains from. It's definitely not from us. Still, after he's finished his schooling at your mysterious academy, I guess that now, because of his new talents, he will get it into his mind to campaign for animal rights, in addition to wanting to change the attitudes of the world in some way or another. Perhaps it will involve the Sciences somehow? I know he loves and has the greatest respect for Charles Darwin."

WD: [Nodding in agreement] "Darwin was a great man." [Suddenly, looking at his watch and papers]. "Well, it's been a pleasure talking to you and your family but it seems that we better make a move. Therefore, I'll leave you to say your goodbyes and then you can have a talk to one of our counsellors about the treatment you'd like to receive."

MS: "No problem. It's been lovely talking to you too and thank you for all you've done to help our family."

[Interview Terminated]

Throughout my reading of this short interview, I spent the whole-time snorting in laughter, although I tried to keep my amusement to a minimal volume because I was afraid that the librarian would come hobbling up here to shout at me. I chuckled violently as I thought about what I had just had the pleasure of reading. This was surely the best part, out of all the documentation to come, although what I later read made me thrilled and amazed to think I had such an incredible ancestor in the family.

After Alistair had graduated the academy, with flying marks in all subjects, especially the Sciences, he went on to become one of the world's top veterinarians and animal rights activists. Alistair was also responsible for influencing millions of new discoveries and opinions on the subject of veterinary medicine and, because of his ability to understand and communicate with animals, he was able to convert others into adopting the vegetarian and/or vegan diet (eventually his parents became vegetarians, which was a fact that made me smile).

More fascinatingly, in his later years, Alistair lived through the terror of World War One, where he worked healing those animals, including horses, who had been injured during battle. It was this time that he suffered the greatest strain, especially after seeing countless horses and men die before his very eyes, due to the severity of their injuries. It also came to light that Alistair was offered a place on the famous ship the 'Titanic' because of his recognised achievements, which tragically sunk in 1912. It was his momentarily ill health that stopped him from boarding the doomed liner although, rather romantically, it was his nurse that he married and later had children with, shortly after falling in love with her thanks to her unwavering patience and kindness. Nonetheless, it was the picture that was taken next to the 'Titanic', which featured my great grandfather and a much younger version of Vladimir Alcaeus, which caused my heart to stop.

My great grandfather was sitting in a wheelchair with his back to the 'Titanic,' looking at an invisible, old fashioned camera. Vladimir Alcaeus was kneeling next to him and, as he too focused on the seemingly, invisible camera, he had that ever-present intelligent sparkle in his eye. When I saw this photo, my hands shook in shock and disbelief. Two major thoughts raced around my head. The first thought was the understanding that clearly, Vladimir and my great grandfather had been extremely close friends. The second thought was the fact that, as Vladimir was obviously alive during that era, this would mean that he was well over a hundred and fifty years old.

Impossible! I thought, staring at the ancient, brown picture in scepticism. *He couldn't be that old. No normal person can live for that long. And yet, it's Vladimir Alcaeus we're talking about here and he's most definitely not normal.*

Taking deep breaths to calm my erratic breathing, I finished reading the file. Then, when I was done, I placed it back on the shelf exactly where I had found it earlier, to ensure that I kept the librarian happy. After all, if I could, I planned to come back here and see if I could find any other interesting files. As I came to the beginning of the shelves, I noticed the surname Alcaeus written in huge, gold fancy writing. My heart skipped a beat. What if I had a look in one of those books, because there were several, bounded by thick clasps and unlocked the secret behind that picture?

Now that, I decided, would be fascinating.

Before I could even touch any of the books, a sharp voice cut through my trance-like state.

"I distinctly remember your permission slip stating that it was for a one Mr. Alistair Silverstone." The librarian barked, fixing me with an unimpressed glare. "Not for a Mr. Vladimir Achilles Alcaeus."

I threw her an embarrassed, guilty look, before mumbling an apology.

"Sorry." I muttered. "I'll be on my way now."

After entering the other half of the library, which seemed to be lighter and airier, I left through the two, gigantic oak doors. As I did so, I felt her constant glare on the back of my neck, until I had sharply turned the corner and was lost from view.

CHAPTER 33: ALEX

I was desperate to tell Jasmine about what I had discovered. However, when she bounded up to me, her face flushed in happiness and delight, I focused my attentions on listening to what she wanted to tell me.

"Oh Alex." She giggled like a besotted lover. "I'm so happy. Raphael's literally just asked me to be his date for the Halloween Ball and obviously, I said yes."

At hearing her words, my heart abruptly plummeted. Nonetheless, I knew I couldn't show these negative emotions. Therefore, I forced a smile on my face and hugged her.

"Aww Jazz." I replied, trying my best to sound happy for her, which I thankfully seemed to pull off. "That's great news."

She giggled again.

"I know right." She answered, clutching her hands together in glee. Her next words were like a horrific, painful punch to my stomach. "Still," she added, "I'm surprised he asked me. I generally thought that he would've asked you to go with him instead." She frowned, before concluding her train of thoughts. "Did he ask you at all?"

Great. I thought. *This was the one thing I had hoped would not happen.*

I did a fantastic result at lying.

"No." I replied, feeling awful inside as I lied. "No. He hasn't brought that topic up with me at all."

As soon as I had answered her, I saw relief flood through her veins.

"Well...thank god for that." She said, sighing. "Otherwise, if he had, it would be seriously awkward between us right now." I thought it better not to answer her. She soldiered on, oblivious. "However, we now need to get you a date for the evening. After all, it's not really very nice going to these events on your own is it?" She giggled again, clearly ecstatic. "Has anyone here taken your fancy?"

At hearing her question, I blushed, wishing the ground could swallow me up for the umpteenth time. Thankfully, Jasmine answered her own question for me, as she continued to babble.

"I suppose Vince from our History class is quite cute - the one who's amazing at running, although he does have help from his speedy powers. Or there's Harry from Geography?" She added. "He took a liking to you the other day when you offered to help him with his diagram on volcanoes. I could read it all over his face." Realising that I wasn't replying to her suggestions and correctly thinking that I was finding this topic uncomfortable (although not for the reasons she believed) she changed direction. "But, moving on from all of that," she now said, "you seemed like you wanted to say something to me before I blurted out my good news. What was it about?"

I shrugged, now feeling cold and numb inside but relieved that she had stopped going on about the Halloween Ball.

"Oh that." I answered. "It doesn't matter. It wasn't important."

At hearing my reply, she looked at me funnily and in the same way she had done yesterday, before we both had gone to bed. Nonetheless, taking my arm, she suddenly pulled me towards the dining hall, for the bell had just gone for lunch.

"God I'm starving." She said. "I hope they've cooked some more of those yummy hot-dogs."

However, I had switched off.

I tried to distract myself with what I had found out about Vladimir and my great grandfather. Somehow, although this sounded an obvious statement, there was more to what I had read than met the eye. What's more, even though I had no way of knowing how to go about it, I was determined to find out as much about both of them as I could, albeit this meant delving into dark waters.

CHAPTER 34: ALEX

*L*unch was unbearably and unbelievably uncomfortable. I sat between Jasmine and Raphael and had to painfully endure listening to Jasmine's discussion of how she wanted to be met outside her room by Raphael and led down the grand staircase like a princess. Overall, I could tell that Raphael wasn't really enjoying the whole situation either. He clearly found the topic of conversation as awkward as I did, despite the fact that Jasmine was oblivious to the whole tense atmosphere. After Jasmine declared that she wanted Raphael to put his arm around her waist, I couldn't take it anymore.
"I'm just going to get my music book before the lesson." I suddenly cried, jumping up unexpectedly and causing Jasmine to look shocked and a bit put out for interrupting her. "I left it in our bedroom."

Raphael went to say something with regards to my abrupt movements and declaration. I shot him a warning look. Now was not the time to start having second thoughts.
"I'll catch you in class." I called out to Jasmine, as I headed out of the dining hall. Then, I ran as far away from the two of them as I possibly could, tears streaming down my face. Oh God. I realised. This whole Halloween Ball, as much as it sounded ridiculous, was beyond awful, even though I knew I couldn't blame Jasmine or Raphael for my hurtling emotions. After all, if I had only accepted Raphael's offer to take me to the Halloween Ball earlier, then my emotions would have been completely different. However, my friendship with Jasmine had ruled all other thoughts at that particular moment in time. What's more, I couldn't turn back time, even if the small, selfish part of me wanted too.
Oh, the joys of being a teenager!

Suddenly, I rounded the corner of a seemingly, empty corridor and barged headfirst into Lucifer. I shouted in alarm as I ended up flying down the hallway, looking like 'Supergirl'. His strong clasp saved me at the last second.

"Hey Alex." Lucifer said, concerned. I frantically scrubbed away my tears. "Are you OK?"

I nodded my head.

"I'll be alright." I answered, trying to smile but it was painful. I had hit my cheek on his iron ribs. "I shouldn't have been charging down the corridor like a raging ball. I hope I haven't hurt you?"

Lucifer shook his head and patted his stomach, subconsciously flexing his muscles to show how strong they were. All I needed to do was paint him green.

"No worries." He replied, smiling. "I'm fine." Nevertheless, deep down, he knew that I was not crying because I was hurt. "Has someone upset you?" Lucifer asked me gently, his features echoing his worry. "Because the look on your face and the tears in your eyes tells me that they have."

It was my turn to shake my head.

"No one's upset me Lucifer." I replied, hastily rubbing away the last of my tears. "Honest. My neck and cheek just hurt from where I bumped into you."

As soon as I had answered him, Lucifer studied me for a minute. From the expression on his features, I could see that he knew I wasn't being truthful with my explanation. After a long drawn out sigh, he decided to change the conversation into something he hoped would brighten the mood. Gradually, his face turned a deep crimson the more he spoke. Little did he know it was on the same topic that had just been causing me grief.

"Hey...em...Alex...em...do you have a date for the Halloween Ball?" He abruptly asked me, blushing shyly whilst we headed off to Music. "Because if you don't, I...I was wondering if you would like to go with me?"

This comment took me by complete surprise.

My mind went into overdrive.

Oh Lucifer, I thought, my heart softening. *You really don't live up to your name at all, but you have such...bad...timing!*

"I'd love to go with you." I heard myself retort, before I could even process what he had just asked me.

Bloody hell. I thought. *Where had that come from?*

When my brain had eventually processed my words, I realised that deep down, I had probably said the right thing.

Lucifer's delighted face said it all really.

"Great." He grinned, looking as if Christmas had just come early. "I'll pick you up about seven thirty if you want?"

I nodded.

"That sounds lovely." I retorted.

For a while, a silence fell between us. The Music room wasn't far away. Soon, I couldn't take the silence any longer. I blurted out something that had come to the forefront of my mind, in Lucifer's presence. It was a secret, rather surprisingly, I had desperately wanted to know more about.

"So...you worked for the RSPCA before you came here then?" I babbled, my face going redder the longer I spoke. "That's cool. What kind of things did you have to do?"

As soon as I had finished talking, Lucifer fixed me with a shocked and terrified stare.

"H...how do you know that?" He stammered, his eyes wild and cautious. "I...I haven't told anyone about that part of my life."

Crap! I thought. I had hoped that Raphael had brought the topic up in discussion with him, seeing as they were dorm mates.

Clearly, I was wrong.

As the fiendish parts of my brain slowly begun to work, I extended the truth to a certain degree.

Awakening

"When we were in our last Music lesson," I told him, trying to keep my face as innocent as possible. "I noticed the leaflet in your bag about the RSPCA as I walked past. Being nosy is kind of a bad habit of mine," I continued, "I'm sorry."

When I had finished speaking, I saw Lucifer's mind go into overdrive, as he digested my excuse. It was a long time before he spoke and, during this process, my realisations that Lucifer was actually, deep down, quite a sensitive, emotional person were heightened further.

With a small, still somewhat wary smile, he nodded.

"That's alright." He finally replied, although he wasn't meeting my gaze and his face was still a profound crimson. "I accept your apology." For another moment, he paused, trying to find the right words. Eventually, he resumed the present topic of conversation. "In answer to your question about what I had to do," he continued, clearly finding each word a struggle. "It was simple really. I worked at a local animal centre, not long after my mother separated from my father, feeding, grooming, socialising and cleaning out the animals. It was such an enjoyable experience and it was my way of relaxing. However," he finalised, "I guess that now, in the future, I'll have to be a little more cautious about where I leave my possessions."

The instant he had finished speaking, I threw Lucifer a puzzled look.

"Why's that?" I asked him, mystified by his comment, especially as I had been listening to the way Lucifer had been talking in quiet reverence. I was honoured by the fact that he was willing to open up to me, considering his misgivings.

"What's so bad about people finding out that you used to work for the RSPCA?"

In answer to my question, Lucifer gestured to himself.

"Do I look like the kind of person who would work with animals?" He retorted, his face filled with a sad honesty. "Many people have their doubts about me, as soon as they see me and your previous facial reaction only succeeded in adding fuel to the fire."

When Lucifer had finished, my heart fell. I realised that I was one of those people who had judged Lucifer due to his size, in addition to his name, before I had even gotten to know him. Now, I realised, he was very different from the person I had perceived him to be. Therefore, I wasn't able to stop the guilt I felt – something that must have showed on my face.

Lucifer acknowledged my reaction to his words with a small, sad nod.

"Your initial reaction only strengthened the reasoning behind why I don't really let anyone in." He said quietly, his eyes expressing his hurt. "To be honest, I can't believe I had the guts to even ask you to go to the Ball with me. Normally, I find it extremely hard to talk to people, especially as they usually treat me with caution. For that reason," he concluded, "I've learnt over the years that it is best if people don't know me - best for others and for me."

It took me a while to process what Lucifer had said. It saddened me greatly to think that, because of his outward appearance, people like me, had viewed Lucifer to be someone he was not. I was also greatly touched by Lucifer's revelations, due to the fact that I had always tried to be someone who didn't conform to society and wanted to be my own individual, unique person. I shook my head, laying a hand supportively on Lucifer's burly shoulder, causing him to shiver.

"Honestly." I told him fiercely. "You're wrong. I think it would be far more beneficial to others and to you if people could know the truth and see the true you." I threw him a sincere smile. "I know it's been beneficial to me to begin to understand what you're really like

Awakening

underneath all that muscle for, deep down," I established, "I've so far come to realise that you're a kind-natured, funny and talented person."

The moment I had finished talking, I saw Lucifer's body stiffen. He looked as if all the muscles, bones and tendons in his body had frozen and it was evident that my words had shocked him. Gradually, the stiffness wore off and he soon gazed at me in profound interest and intrigue.

"You really believe that?" He finally asked me in a hushed whisper, his eyes shining with a newly found sense of understanding.

I nodded, smiling at him.

"Yes, I do." I replied, still smiling at him kindly. "And I'm sure everyone else would too if you only allowed them to see more of who you really are, rather than pretending to be someone you're not."

I could tell from the look on Lucifer's face that my words had struck a chord deep within him. My words seemed to not only change the way he viewed himself, but also appeared to have changed the way he viewed me. It was then that I realised we were now standing outside the Music room. Lucifer also realised our present location and, with a small, shy smile, he gestured for me to go first.

As we entered the room, we were both filled with an inner, emotional awakening, especially as I realised that perhaps I could get through the Halloween Ball after all now. It would still be difficult, considering the whole "Raphael" scenario. However, at least going with Lucifer would make the situation more bearable.

CHAPTER 35: ALEX

When I entered the Music room with Lucifer, Jasmine looked up from our usual table and called out to me across the classroom, concern written all over her face.

"I've been so worried about you." She cried, as I made my way over to where she was sitting. "The way you suddenly got up and went earlier made me think I'd done something wrong."

I did my best to hold back my jumble of thoughts at hearing her comment and forced a weak smile.

"It wasn't to do with you at all."

I saw her breathe out a sigh of relief.

"Good." Jasmine smiled, before she continued. "Did you manage to get your Music book?" she asked me. "Was it in our dorm room?"

Now, throughout the entirety of our conversation, Lucifer had stood nearby, quietly unpacking his own equipment. After he overheard our conversation, particularly the last comment, he threw me a knowing look which I met and said: "I knew that you were lying to me earlier about someone upsetting you. The fact that you were far from the dormitories speaks volumes." Unfortunately, Jasmine spotted our exchanged glances and put two and two together, but in a different way than was intended.

"Oooo...Lucifer seems to be quite smitten with you." She giggled, throwing me an intrigued glance. "I saw you two come in earlier together, but never twigged something might be going on. Go on," she added, "spill the juicy beans."

I blushed, after she had spoken, which only confirmed her suspicions. In a small, muted voice, I told her about the Halloween Ball. However, I decided not to tell her anything else about Lucifer's disclosures, because I wanted him to reveal all to her (and hopefully others) in his own time.

"It's nothing really." I replied, muttering in a hushed voice so not to embarrass Lucifer. "Lucifer only asked me to be his date to the Halloween Ball."

Jasmine's squawk of delight obliterated my intentions, for I saw Lucifer's cheeks begin to go pink, as he realised what had been said.
"Aww Alex." She giggled excitedly. "That's wonderfully cute. Now the four of us can go as a double date."

I didn't answer her, to save Lucifer and me from further embarrassment. Throughout the entirety of the lesson, Lucifer and I did our best to ignore each other, for fear of experiencing more of Jasmine's unbelievably loud, humiliating giggles. I also didn't want to anger Miss Crotchet, who had already given Jasmine and I a warning about gossiping in her lesson. When the bell went, signifying the time for our final lesson, Lucifer and I kept a large distance between us, as the two of us left the classroom, with Jasmine following shortly behind.

"I'll see you later." I told her as I headed off to Power Control, watching Lucifer leave through the corner of my eye. "Good luck with your History test." She nodded, her tight, curly hair bouncing up and down, before shooting me a grateful smile.

"Thanks." She called back. "I'll need it."

Then, we parted ways, walking off in different directions.

CHAPTER 36: ALEX

I'll emphasise once more how awesome Power Control was. This was for many reasons, although the main one can be left to your imagination. In today's lesson, since Mr Allen had now experienced a preview of our talents and control over them so far, he had set each of us individual tasks to carry out. He explained at the beginning of the lesson that we had two key focuses.

The first focus included the fact that all of us didn't need to close our eyes to use our powers. Instead, we just needed to feel and learn to become one with them. Mr Allen told us that this was something which we could practise at any time, such as sitting down quietly in our dorm rooms and listening to the recognisable call of our powers, which varied from person to person. The second focus was mostly aimed at Blaze and me. Unlike Gretel and Ivy, who were constantly surrounded by their elements, Blaze and I usually had to rely heavily on hoping that our element was nearby. Therefore, although there were water objects in the room, as well as a lake outside to practise on once I had fully mastered my powers, this fact made it difficult for us to channel and use our powers. Mr Allen had a way to help us with this situation. This way was harder than most people could imagine and, in his opinion, made our powers the most difficult to control and use. After all, to succeed, Mr Allen told us that we had to learn how to control and create our powers with thought alone. However, in his opinion, once mastered, this method would ensure ultimate success.

After seeing to Gretel, who had set to work practising her talent in a specially constructed side room and Ivy, who was now seated in a pretend garden area in the far side of the classroom, Mr Allen set to work training us.

"It took me many, many years of hard work, dedication and patience until I reached the level I'm now at." He explained, demonstrating this statement with effortless ease. His element swirled about the area we were working in, created with just his mind. "What's more," he continued, "after I had mastered controlling my power with thought alone, it took me even longer until I could control it well. Therefore, don't expect to be able to do this immediately." We both nodded, fully understanding what he had said, before he finalised his introductory speech. "Both of you are extremely talented," he stated, smiling at us warmly. "However, like the others, you've a long way to go until you can leave this academy, free of the fears that you will harm others in any shape, way or form. That being said, let's begin."

Once Mr Allen had finished his introduction, he set to work positioning us so that we were sitting on the ground facing him.
Then, our training commenced.
"First things first," he began, "I want you to try and switch off all your senses apart from touch and sight, but don't close your eyes as you do this, even though that sounds impossible." I was surprised by this comment. It sounded like a strange and unmanageable thing to do. Mr Allen smiled at me reassuringly and my body automatically relaxed. Gosh, he had such a lovely smile. "That's right." He nodded at me. "Maximum relaxation is vital. Now, once you're completely at ease, gradually switch off your senses, until touch and sight are all that remain. Take it slowly." He instructed. "Imagine that you have all the time in the world."

Initially, I'm not going to lie, I struggled with this. It was hard to relax and concentrate, especially when Ivy and Gretel were grunting in frustration and I could smell the faint wafts of dinner floating under the classroom door. To make matters harder, Blaze seemed to be able to pick up this step quicker than I could, so much so that his beaming smile made me feel quite jealous.

Mr Allen's voice disrupted my envious thoughts.

"Relax." He said, smiling encouragingly and looking at me. "Just relax and allow yourself to feel and embrace your power."

Following his instructions, I allowed myself to switch off my senses, whilst keeping somewhat awake and alert as I did so. As soon as this happened, bit by bit, I felt the electrical charge, which constantly whizzed about inside me, become stronger by the second. The noise level in the room dimmed and the smell of dinner slowly became non-existent. In the end, as my sight and touch intensified, the electric charge ultimately turned into glorious, overpowering warmth. It was as if my body was burning up, but it wasn't an uncomfortable sensation.

In actual fact, it was the opposite.

As I became overwhelmed with this wonderful warmth, I caught Mr Allen's eye and I saw him gesturing at me, wanting to bring me back to reality. Therefore, with a nod, I allowed my power to return to its usual strength, until it became once more a gentle tingle.

Mr Allen beamed at Blaze and I.

"Wow." He said, his voice filled with admiration and respect. "The two of you picked that tricky task up so quickly. It normally takes others far more attempts to achieve what you just did."

At hearing this news, Blaze and I exchanged pleased glances. Realising our potential, Mr Allen decided to take the whole situation one step further.

"OK." He spoke again, bringing us back to attention. "Now that I've seen what the two of you are capable of, let's try and see if we can take this lesson to the next level. Therefore," he instructed, "I want you to enter that same zone again but, when you do, I want you to grasp hold of the power you feel and try to visually project it, without closing your eyes. Do you understand me?"

Blaze and I nodded. Then, we followed his instructions meticulously. It took me a long time and many failed attempts to once again master the art of switching on and off my other senses. By the end, I realised that Blaze was now the one struggling, although I put this down to the nature of his unpredictable powers. When I felt that familiar rush of electric pulse and realised that I was completely in tune with it, I relaxed my body, until my powers passed over me like a soothing, warm wave.
Instantly, I knew we were one.

Slowly, ignoring everything else around me and concentrating entirely on my own task, I listened to the call of my powers. A rich, beautiful, jubilant melody filled my mind and, as soon as I noticed it, I tried to grab hold of it. It slipped and slid like liquid between my mental hands, refusing to obey my command. What's more, my powers behaved like a naughty child, constantly changing direction and trying to hide in the darkest corners of my mind. Nevertheless, I refused to be beaten, despite the fact that I could hear Mr Allen faintly suggesting that I call it a day, especially as Blaze had decided to stop.
Giving up was just not in my DNA.

Suddenly, my mental fingers grasped the core of my powers, which was a vibrant blue and green and I was overwhelmed with the salty, smell of the ocean.
The result was incredible.

As soon as I had contacted my powers, my body exploded in electricity and heat, which was reflected in the swirling, ocean colours of my eyes. As my powers and I met each other properly for the first time, I sensed that, deep down, there was more to them than met the eye. All the same, concentrating, I pushed myself, willing my powers to do as I mentally commanded. Water suddenly formed from thin air, swirling about me like a raging current. All this happened in only a few seconds, although, to me, it felt like an eternity of glory. I laughed, delighted with what was happening and proud of my achievements, as a sparkling waterfall was created before my very eyes.

As soon as this amazing creation had been born, my powers began to buck wildly. It was as if they had a mind of their own. As I tried to tame them, I heard Mr Allen's voice once more, in the far distance. He was shouting. As soon as Mr Allen's sharp voice met my ears, my concentration broke, just like it had done previously. In an instant, the water, which I had created, fell to the ground, soaking Blaze and Mr Allen, yet again, from head to toe. After the ringing in my ears had subsided, I met their shocked and somewhat terrified faces with an equally surprised and fearful look.

Blaze was the first one to speak.

"A...Alex." He whispered, although his voice sounded like it had been magnified a million times over in the deathly silence. "A...are you alright?"

Slowly, I nodded, before blushing red.

"I...I'm so, so sorry." I abruptly burst out, unable to contain the jumble of mixed emotions rocketing around my body. "I...I didn't mean –"

Mr Allen cut me off with a wave of his hand.

"No apologies are needed." Mr Allen said, once he had managed to close his gaping mouth and wring out his t-shirt. "Although I think that everyone has had enough training for today."

The moment Mr Allen had finished, I dropped my eyes, trying to slow my still frantically beating heart. My fellow classmates groaned in disappointment at hearing this news. Once the others had started to tidy up and collect their things ready to go down to dinner, Mr

Allen motioned for me to step outside. Feeling my blush deepen, I followed him and three pairs of eyes tracked my every movement. It was only when we were out of sight and ear shot, that Mr Allen let loose his real emotions on the matter.

"Alex." Mr Allen muttered, swallowing profusely, unsure about how to approach the subject in question. After taking many deep breaths, he continued. "I'm not really sure about how to say this but I'm both frightened and mesmerised by your talent." I gave him a small smile at hearing his words and let out a sigh of relief. After all, I had thought that I was going to be in huge trouble for what I had just done. Seeing his genuinely astonished stare made me blush further. "The extent of your power is like nothing I or anyone else has ever witnessed in a long time. Therefore," he continued, "knowing this information has got me thinking if you would like personal training sessions?"

At this news, my eyes lit up, for I couldn't have thought of a more perfect way of spending my days training with this superhot teacher. It was as if all my dreams had come true. Clearly reading my mind, which caused me to go an even darker red, he explained all in far greater detail.

"The lessons wouldn't be with me," he chuckled, "although I'd be more than happy to train you. No. I was thinking more of having personal training sessions with Vladimir Alcaeus. Then, you'd be receiving the best in the business!"

My heart fluttered.

Now, that was the kind of offer you couldn't refuse, although it was a shame not to be taught by Mr Allen. I had often fantasised about having a one on one lesson with him. Painfully ignoring that enjoyable thought, I accepted his offer.

"That would be amazing." I heard myself answer in a breathy tone. "Only if Vladimir would be willing to train me that is?"

Mr Allen smiled.

"I'm sure he would be only too happy to oblige." He replied. "After all, outstanding talent like yours is something that I know, for a fact, he wouldn't say no to."

After hearing the last of his words, I agreed that, if Vladimir was willing to train me, then I was more than willing to accept what was being offered. Mr Allen was delighted by this confirmation, a fact emphasised by his glowing grin and his vigorous shaking of my hand, as we made the deal. Then, the two of us returned back to the training room. As soon as Mr Allen and I re-entered the classroom, the bell went, signalling the end of the lesson. This noise was met with a small groan from all of us. Once I had collected my things, Gretel, Blaze, Ivy and I set off to dinner, excitedly talking about what had just happened. As we walked, I eventually asked Blaze about his background.

"So..." I asked him. "How did you end up here, in England?"

Blaze met my question with a small, knowing smile.

"It was my parents' idea actually." He chuckled. "They met when my father, who's English and a successful businessman, was on holiday, touring the Canadian Rockies. My mother was a local guide, who lived in the town of Jasper and it was love at first sight." He continued, laughing. "As soon as my father was due to return home, he arranged for my mother to fly back to England with him. They couldn't keep their hands off each other and, naturally, one thing led to another." He finalised. "That's why I'm here."

At hearing his last comment, a small smile passed over my lips, especially as Blaze waggled his eyebrows shrewdly up and down.

I wasn't done interrogating him.

"Surely you must regret not being able to see the Canadian scenery and live alongside its wildlife on a daily basis?" I asked him. "I mean, it's not like you have the chance to see a moose or a grizzly bear here every day! Therefore, really," I concluded, "in comparison to Canada, British wildlife is pretty lame."

At hearing my comment, Blaze laughed harder than he had done previously.

"You do know that only happens in certain areas of the country and I'd most likely feel shock, both on the animal's part and mine, as opposed to excitement, if that happened!" He retorted, noting my amused expression. "At least here, the only dangerous animal you might face is an ill-tempered fox or a stray cat. All the same," he finalised, "it would be pretty cool, I suppose, although I do travel to Canada every summer to see my mother's half of the family - the ones she abandoned for love."

When Blaze had finished telling his life-story, I shot him a small smile. His tale was actually rather wonderful and, as long as his parents and he were happy, then that was all that mattered. Eventually, the two of us parted ways and, whilst I headed off to console my rumbling stomach, I hoped my story would have a similar, fairy-tail ending.

CHAPTER 37: HECATE

Not a moment after Alexandra had gone, Hecate stepped out of her hiding place.

"Has the offer been made?" She abruptly asked Mr Allen, fixing his enchanted stare with a piercing gaze of her own.

Mr Allen nodded.

"Of course it has." He smiled, before he took her pale hand in his and lightly kissed it. "I'd never let you down."

Hecate blushed in his presence, which was one of the few times she had reddened in a long time. The colour in her cheeks went as quickly as it had come and she managed to master her icy composure once more, sort of.

"Good." She retorted, although her usual frostiness had somewhat melted in Mr Allen's presence. "I'll give Vladimir the excellent news." Hecate then went to leave.

Mr Allen held her back.

"Are you going to the Halloween Ball?" He asked her, grinning. "If you are, then I'd love to take you." This news startled Hecate. It had been so unexpected that she gasped a little, her pale lips parting slightly.

At hearing Mr Allen's request, Hecate threw him a flirtatious glance, which he met with surprise. Instantly, Hecate felt delighted with the momentary freedom it gave her to be the person she secretly was deep down, despite the fact that she had suffered so much heartache over the years.

"I'd like that very much Ian." She answered him, using his first name, which caused him to shiver. "It's very kind of you to even ask me."

Despite his obvious delight at her acceptance and tone, Mr Allen wasn't done.

"What are you going as?" Mr Allen asked her eagerly, as soon as she had finished. "I was thinking of going as 'Dracula'."

Hecate laughed at this comment, once more warmth flooding through her, which only ever seemed to happen in Mr Allen's presence.

"I can definitely see that costume suiting you." She retorted, chuckling. "Although I do hope you won't be drinking anyone's blood that night. As for me," Hecate flashed him a beautiful smile. "I'll be going as myself of course. I'm surprised you even had to ask."

At hearing her answer, Mr Allen threw her the biggest beam in the world, before he lowered his voice. It was deep and passionate. Hecate shivered in uncontrollable pleasure.

"Oh...there's only one person I've got in mind whom I wish to drink the blood of." He whispered seductively, winking. "And I'm sure they know who they are."

Once more, Hecate trembled in delight at his words. Oh, how this man could thaw even the iciest of hearts. Mr Allen was also the only other person, apart from Vladimir, who didn't seem to mind that her powers were to communicate with the dead or was frightened by the terrible stories that had always haunted her past. They plagued her, like a bad omen.

As Hecate grinned back at him, deep down, she realised that she was the kind of woman who enjoyed leaving men wanting more. She liked teasing them and watching their reactions. Therefore, with a swish of her black, lace skirt, which caused her hand to suddenly drop from his, making Mr Allen gasp, she began walking away from him, her normal frosty composure once again appearing on her face. However, so that she could show him that she was still interested, Hecate turned and smiled flirtatiously. She swayed her hips, feeling a spark of happiness ignite within her, when she caught his thrilled and relieved expression. Then, with a twirl, she was swallowed up by the night.

CHAPTER 38: ALEX

I was summoned by Vladimir not long after dinner had ended. Raphael, Jasmine and I had been making our way tiredly to bed, when a note was thrust sharply into my hand, by a passing pupil, who was clearly one of the student messengers. Jasmine, Raphael and I stepped to one side to allow the other pupils to pass easily by, before I opened the note in both eager and nervous anticipation.
This is what it read:

Dear Alexandra Raven,

I'm delighted to hear that you wish to have personal training sessions with me. Therefore, please could you report to my office at precisely 8:00pm, as I feel we should become acquainted with one other before our training sessions begin?

Kind regards,
Vladimir Alcaeus

As they both read the note's contents over my quivering shoulder, Jasmine was the first person to voice her opinion.
"What training sessions?" She asked me in a confused and somewhat indignant tone of voice. "You've not said anything to Raphael or me about you having personal training sessions with Vladimir Alcaeus."

I blushed after hearing her accusation. I hadn't told either of them about this news because really, it was a private matter and one I didn't want everyone to know about. From the loudness of Jasmine's voice though, I feared that my wish had abruptly been rejected.

"Alex doesn't have to tell us everything that goes on in her life you know Jazz." Raphael's voice seemed to cut through the increasing, heavy atmosphere, causing Jasmine's mouth to open and close, but no sound to be heard.

I threw him an appreciative glance. In the end, feeling the growing tension, I pulled them down a quiet corridor and told them about what had happened, in a hushed whisper.

"Basically," I began, "I've been offered personal training sessions by Vladimir because my Power Control teacher seems to think that I'd benefit from them. However, I'd be really grateful if this news does not get spread around the school. You know the kind of spiteful damage it could do."

Jasmine threw me a jealous look after listening to my explanation, which wounded me significantly. Despite registering my hurt, Jasmine's surprising resentment got the better of her.

"So...you're essentially telling me that you're better than us now are you?" Jasmine retorted unkindly.

At hearing this uncalled for comment, I gasped, my face betraying my hurt and shock. Her cutting tone hit me like a ton of bricks. Trying to control my turmoil of emotions, I answered her in the calmest voice I could muster.

"No." I retorted. "No. I'm not saying that at all and I've had nothing to do with this. It's my Power Control teacher who's organised the whole thing."

Jasmine still found a reason to spitefully pick at me.

"But you're still agreeing to this situation. Therefore, that means that you're involved in this decision."

After she had finished talking, I looked at her stunned, unable to believe what I was hearing. Surely, like Raphael, she should be *happy* for me, not showing off like an envious bitch?

Feeling my hurt and annoyance explode, I didn't hold back.

"Well...excuse me for wanting to make the most out of the opportunities put before me." I retorted sarcastically, now feeling hot tears fall from my eyes. "I think that if you were in my shoes, you'd have done the same thing. However," I finalised, "I know that I wouldn't have replied so horribly if it had been my closest friend who had been offered such a wonderful opportunity."

Jasmine paled at this retort, realising her wrongdoing. Nonetheless, I was so mad at her now that I unleashed all my emotions and thoughts, not really caring whether people could hear my rant. The green-eyed monster also got the better of me.

"Oh, and another thing." I added frostily. "Raphael did ask me to be his date for the Halloween Ball, before he asked you, but I turned...him...down because I didn't want to betray our friendship." This last piece of news was a bombshell for Jasmine, whose face flickered with numerous emotions, including anger, hurt, regret and embarrassment. She glared at Raphael with a heated expression.

Ignoring her completely, Raphael just focused his entire attention on me, his golden eyes filled with anguish, as if my words had just reopened many wounds. I was not in the mood to be in their presence anymore. Taking no notice of either of them, although I guessed that much would be said after I had gone, I turned sharply on my heel and stormed off in a flurry of rage and bitterness towards Vladimir's office.

CHAPTER 39: ALEX

I had barely knocked on the door when Vladimir called out to me and thanked me for coming. Trying my best to tame my hurtling emotions, I stepped into his office, which caused me to gasp in amazement.

"It's quite something isn't it?" Vladimir asked me, as I carefully made my way up to his desk, doing my best to avoid the numerous ancient and unusual looking artefacts, which crowded around my feet.

I nodded in reply to his question, gazing in wonder around the vast room, before my eyes found his. When they did, I felt as if he was searching me.

No need to panic. Vladimir's voice sounded in my head, causing me to gasp involuntary. He merely smiled. *I promise that I won't hurt you. I just want to take a look into your past.*

Without knowing why, although this news sounded terrifying, my body immediately relaxed at the sound of his calm, steady tone. I felt my mind slacken. Instantly, Vladimir was scanning my recollections. Vladimir started with my first memories as a toddler, crawling around my parents' original, rundown apartment, giggling excitedly as I watched a spider crawl across the carpet. Suddenly, I put it in my mouth. My mother's shouts of: "No darling...no we don't eat spiders. Oh Christ – that's disgusting!" could be heard before Vladimir fast forwarded my childhood, skipping to the day when I had first started Primary school.

I was standing alone, feeling upset and wishing that I could just go home and play with my toys. Suddenly, I was being asked if I wanted to play a game of 'It' by a boy my age, who had messy, ginger hair and big, green eyes. At hearing his request, I was shy at first, for I pulled away from him and sort comfort from the rough, wooden play post nearby. After another gentle offer, I slowly

Awakening

nodded, sensing that this boy was just trying to be friendly. Soon, my thoughts became positive, for I was laughing delightedly, as I knew that I had just made my first wonderful and probably only friend. David had always been so lovely to me since that day. Now though, I didn't know if our friendship was intact, after delivering my shocking disclosure many weeks ago.

Swiftly, this happy memory faded and I was now being chased by Jessica Wademen and her cronies. I ducked behind the school bins, but they found me and threw paint all over my nice, new, clean, school uniform. It had taken me hours to remove the paint stains, so that my parents wouldn't have to know and worry about me being bullied. However, that memory abruptly became dark and now I saw myself on the day of my 'awakening', water streaming out of my fingertips and surrounding Jessica in a watery cocoon. It had felt so wonderful to finally have payback. Subsequently, Jack's face appeared, telling me about my powers, before this memory changed to one of me learning about my great grandfather. Then, I saw David's heartbroken and frightened face, after I had told him about my newly found powers. Finally, Vladimir raced through other more current memories concerning Jasmine, Raphael and Hecate, before everything went black.

I found myself back in his office, now feeling completely and utterly exposed after such a peculiar experience. Vladimir just grinned, after he had finished and looked at me as if I was some long hoped for prize.

She must be connected to Mortimer somehow. Vladimir thought to himself, as he flicked through Alexandra's memories. *Such unbelievable bravery, strength of mind and willfulness. Plus, I can sense tremendous power within and all around her, much like Hecate picked up on.*

As Vladimir became lost in his excited thoughts, unaware of his quiet reverie, I was bewitched when my eyes fell on the dagger sitting directly behind him. As soon as my eyes rested on such an enchanting object, I felt as if I had to restrain myself from racing over to the cabinet, smashing the glass and claiming it as my own. It was as if it had me under some kind of spell.

The dagger called to me in a virtually inaudible, soft, throbbing hum and its blood red jewel drew me in, enticing me to take the hilt and complete the duty it was destined to fulfil. Vladimir's voice suddenly broke my trance, bringing me back to reality.
"Do you hear the song too?" He asked me in a breathy tone, gesturing to the dagger. "It's so quiet and yet, it's always present."

Slowly, unsure of why I did it, I nodded.
"Yes." I muttered. "Yes, I can hear its faint, melancholy tune. It's extremely soft and yet, if you listen hard enough, it is there."

Vladimir nodded. Even Hecate had not heard the call of the dagger, although she had been affected by it like many others, whom had visited him. The fact that this girl, Alexandra, could hear its call, just like Vladimir himself, spoke volumes and confirmed his suspicions.

Vladimir motioned at me to leave him to his troubled thoughts.
"I'll call for you soon," Vladimir told me, "and we'll start our training. However, for now, I want you to practise your powers to the best of your ability, for you're extraordinarily gifted."

I nodded, feeling both confused and scared, as I watched Vladimir in silence. He slowly became consumed by dark contemplations. As I closed the door quietly behind me and saw Vladimir watching me in interest, the dagger called out to me. Its strange tune filled my mind once more and I knew that, one day, I wouldn't be able to resist its all-too-powerful call.

CHAPTER 40: ALEX

I was terribly nervous as I returned to my dorm, so much so that my hands were actually dripping with sweat. This anxiety was because I had no idea how Jasmine was feeling since our argument. I also felt the swirl of dark emotions reappear in my heart, as I recalled her jealous words. When I opened the door, I was immediately jumped on by Jasmine, who threw her arms around me and virtually squeezed the life out of me. I noticed how her eyes were sore and extremely red.

She began to sob uncontrollably.

"O...oh A...Alex." She stammered, in-between sobs. "I h...have been the...the w...worst f...friend e...ever." She gurgled. Inside, I sighed. Clearly, she wasn't the kind of person who seemed to hold grudges. "I...I h...have been such...such a...a moo!"

"It's OK." I replied gently, feeling my heart soften. I took out a box of Kleenex tissues and gave them to her, for she had a disgustingly, runny nose. Looking into her eyes, I saw the sincerity in them. She was generally upset by her earlier unkind behaviour. "I forgive you."

Jasmine threw me a thankful smile, before blowing her nose on one of the hankies I had given her.

Then, she continued to stammer.

"I...I had no idea about you...you and Raphael." She said. "If I had...had k...known that you I...liked each o...other then I wouldn't h...have accepted his o...offer to take...take me to...to the H...Halloween Ball s...so quickly and...and w...without talk...talking t...to you f...first. A...also," she added, "I h...have been so...so unkind, in particular my c...comments earlier about y...your p...private lessons with V...Vladimir. I h...hope it all went w...well today?"

I gave her hand a gentle squeeze.

"Look." I answered softly. "All that's happened between the three of us has been said and done now and we'll forget about it, although yes thanks, the session I had with Vladimir was alright, if not a little strange. However," I continued, "regarding the Halloween Ball, we can still go as a double date...can't we?" I tried to see the brighter side of the situation, as well as comfort her. "After all, I'm still going to the Halloween Ball with Lucifer."

Jasmine shook her head sadly.

"That's not going to happen now Alex." She said, her eyes once more brimming with tears. "Raphael and I had a huge argument about the matter, not long after you left and it ended on both of us agreeing that it was best if we didn't go together."

At hearing her answer, the devil inside of me danced delightedly, surprising me. I tried to push these dark emotions down, desperate to hide them in front of Jasmine. My plan seemed to work for, as soon as I saw how disappointed Jasmine was, I set to work thinking about how to rectify the situation. As far as I was aware, most people seemed to have found dates now, especially as the Halloween Ball was virtually upon us. I knew this because gossip came in handy now and again, when I could be bothered to eavesdrop. Suddenly, an idea came to me. Not long after I had sent him a text, Lucifer knocked on my door.

I opened it up cautiously.

"So...I got your text." He said, smiling slightly, although it looked somewhat strained. "I don't mind taking the two of you if it helps to solve any problems."

At hearing his answer, I threw him the biggest, thankful glance in the world. He was such a gentleman and kind-hearted person.

I vowed to never be judgmental again.

"You have no idea how much this means to me." I told him, as he looked at me with a sad expression. "And how much it will mean to Jazz when she finds out."

Lucifer blushed at my words. At the sound of her name, Jasmine abruptly appeared by my shoulder.
"Oh Lucifer." She said, surprised. "What are you doing here?"
He explained his intentions.
"Well...Alex briefly told me what had happened and asked if I'd be willing to take both of you to the Halloween Ball, instead of just her. I've come to tell you that I've accepted her request. After all," he added, "I'd never decline a friend help, plus refuse the company of two, beautiful women. That would just be unheard of."

After Lucifer had finished, Jasmine threw me a surprised look, filled with both deepest regret and poignant friendship.
"Oh Alex. Did you really do this to help me?" She asked, unable to believe her ears.
I nodded.
"Yes," I replied. "I know how much you wanted someone to take you to the Halloween Ball, so I decided that you could share my date, with his approval of course. Fortunately, he's agreed to take two girls for the price of one."

I tried to lighten the atmosphere. Luckily, this happened. Jasmine once again threw her arms around me.
"I'll never say such uncalled for and unkind things to you again." She exclaimed, pinkie-promising me, once she had grabbed my little finger. "You're the best friend a girl like me could ever ask for."
I returned her hug, before saying goodbye to Lucifer.
"Thanks for what you've done." I told him, when Jasmine had gone back into our room. "It means so much to me."
Lucifer just nodded.

"I know it does." He said. His next words caught me off guard. "But I mostly did it because I wanted to help you. I could tell from your frantic text that you were upset and, after what you did for me, it was the least I could do. I hope that you're alright now."
I nodded.
"I'm fine," I told him, "and I'll see you around."
Lucifer smiled.
"See you both soon and remember, at seven thirty, I'll be right here, waiting for you." Then, he turned around and left a weary and emotionally confused me behind him.

CHAPTER 41: ALEX

The morning of the Halloween Ball, I checked my e-mail, doing my best to try and forget my troubled thoughts. Jasmine and Raphael had been refusing to talk to each another since their argument and Raphael had even rebuffed my gaze, during the few times we had conversed, leading up to today.

As I opened my 'inbox', I forgot my troubles, as I excitedly realised that I had a reply from my parents. Opening the e-mail, I read the contents with mixed emotions.

From: Cathy&Toby@btinternet.com
To: Alex4chocolate@btinternet.com
Date: 29th October 2015
Time: 4:56pm
Subject: Hi Baby!

Hi baby,

Oh honey, it's so wonderful to hear from you and all about your time at the academy so far. Your father and I are so proud of you. The grounds you describe are very famous. I believe your ancestors talked about them numerous times when they were at the academy, especially your great grandfather - Alistair. I'm sure he loved the great lake most of all when he was studying there.

With regards to you being allowed to do some ancestry digging, it sounds so exciting and I suggest that you follow through with this offer. As your great grandfather was so very famous, much was written about his work and personal history. Unfortunately, we "normal" persons are not allowed to access those documents. Therefore, those sources are precious and invaluable, so make the most of it and do let us know what you find out in due course if you can.

What's more, your Music teacher sounds wonderful — just the kind of person I'd love to meet and so does this Mr Allen. He comes across as being extremely dreamy and that part of your letter made me laugh the most, although your father just rolled his eyes, as you can imagine. As for the other teachers you talked about, particularly the ones you don't like so much, just try to cope with them to the best of your ability. The teacher you named as Miss Beast clearly has her own style of teaching and personality, which works for her (but understandably not others) and I know that you'll keep calm as much as you can. Just please promise me that you won't do anything to annoy her (not that you would ever dream of doing this) because I really don't want to hear that you're lying in hospital, with a body full of broken bones.

In terms of Hecate, be on your guard. From what you say, she does sound rather peculiar. However, if she was a serious threat to any of the students at the academy, including you, then Vladimir Alcaeus would never have hired her. He's one of the most trustworthy and respectable men alive. For that reason, I've and so has your father got complete faith in his choice of staff at the academy.

The last three topics you discussed in your original e-mail included the girl Vanessa, your brother and David. In terms of Vanessa, there're always girls like her in every school. Consequently, the best advice I can give you is to just take no notice of her comments as much as possible. However, should she start to bully you, then please let a member of staff know. As for your brother and David, Matthew is fine. He's gradually coming to terms with what has happened to you, although it's a slow progress. Nevertheless, David's been acting quite distant. I happened to see him recently but,

Awakening

as soon as he saw me, he crossed the road as if I was some kind of leper. I don't know what happened between the two of you but, if you told him about your 'awakening', then David seems to have taken the news badly. All the same, I'll continue to keep an eye on him and make sure that he doesn't do anything rash.
Much love and hugs always,
Mum and Dad xxxxx

This last news about David sent my world rocketing. I had hoped and prayed that since telling him about my powers, he would soon come to terms with what had happened. I had always thought that our friendship had been strong enough to cope with my revelations. Clearly though, he was in a bad way and I prayed that my Mum was able to keep him safe and free from harm.

As for my brother, I was pleased to hear that he was coming to terms with what had happened, despite his slow progress. After all, his reaction, I could see now, was understandable and I was thankful that hopefully, one day, when I would see him again, we could put this incident behind us and move on.

Suddenly, Jasmine came over to me, looking pale and told me that Raphael was asking to see me outside. Throwing her a supportive glance and logging out of my account, I swallowed as I opened the door.
Raphael stood there, twiddling his thumbs.

As soon as he saw me, after I had closed the door carefully behind me, he blushed.
"Hey." He said, his golden eyes filling with nerves. "How're you doing?"
I threw him an awkward glance, my heart hammering.
So...after basically ignoring me for a century, you've decided to talk to me now have you?

"I'm alright I guess." I replied, not really knowing what else to say.

Luckily, he seemed to take the bull by the horns.

"So..." He mumbled. "Lucifer told me this morning about his plans for the Halloween Ball. I had no idea that you'd decided to go with him as his date."

I nodded.

"Yes, I did." I replied, leaning uncomfortably against the wall. "When you agreed to go to the Halloween Ball with Jasmine, Lucifer asked me to be his date not long afterwards and I accepted." Raphael's face darkened a little at my explanation. Nevertheless, I continued, wanting to update him about my plans for this evening. "However, with that being said, tonight Jasmine and I are both Lucifer's dates now. I planned the whole thing yesterday, when the two of you had an argument."

At this comment, he stiffened in cold remembrance. Then, rather abruptly, Raphael took my hand and closed the gap between us, so that his golden eyes burned fiercely into mine.

My heart beat wildly in my chest.

"I...I called the whole thing off." He replied, his voice husky and trembling slightly. "Because, when you told Jasmine yesterday about me asking you to be my date, I saw in your eyes just how much you like me." He closed the gap between our faces even more, so that our lips were almost touching. "I feel the same way." He cried, looking at me with a pleading expression. "Therefore, I came to ask you to be my date. We were meant to go together from the beginning and I'm begging you now, for the second time, to let fate take its course!"

My heart stopped beating.

It took me a while to make up my mind, as an internal battle raged within me. On the one hand, for so long, even after what had happened yesterday, I had wondered if it was still possible for this situation to occur. Clearly, my wishes had been heard. I knew that Raphael and I shared an instant attraction from the moment we had locked gazes, something that he had now admitted to me and to our own hearts. Also, throughout the time we had spent together, I had felt this attraction gradually strengthen in desire and ferocity. We were so like one another, both in a negative and positive sense.

On the other hand, I realised that if I said "yes", then this answer would be unfair on Lucifer and Jasmine. It could leave a massive dent in our friendship – a friendship that had already taken a serious beating. Subsequently, dreading what was to come, I met Raphael's intense gaze, shaking with numerous emotions.

"Oh Raphael." I whispered, feeling the electric charge that had formed between the two of us surge throughout my body at his touch. "I...I do I...like you. I...I like you...a lot." Every word was said with shaky breaths. They were like blows to my body. "But," I choked out. "I can't refuse to go with Lucifer and break up my arrangement with Jasmine. It would be unfair at such a late notice."

As I slowly revealed my final decision, Raphael's whole body tensed. I saw the hurt and anger build steadily in his beautiful, golden eyes like a gigantic storm swell. Neither of us spoke, as Raphael and I tried to come to terms with my rejection for the second time, although it was agonisingly painful. God, I felt so awful. Every molecule of my body screamed at me to take my words back.

In the end, Raphael nodded briskly.

"Fine." He muttered coldly under his breath, his face becoming scarily impassive after a show of turbulent emotions. "Fine." Then, heartbreakingly, without a single glance in my direction, he turned and walked dejectedly away...again.

CHAPTER 42: ALEX

I could tell that Jasmine was eager to know about why Raphael had visited our dorm. However, I told her that our original plan for Lucifer to take the two of us to the Halloween Ball still stood, which calmed down her anxiety and curiosity. As the time came to get ready for the Halloween Ball, after our morning lessons and lunch had finished (which worryingly Raphael didn't turn up for) we set to work preparing ourselves and our outfits. To be fair to Jasmine, she looked gorgeous in her cat costume, which consisted of sparkly, black hot pants, a glittery, black t-shirt and a long tail, made from scrunched tights, with a pink bow on the end. She had also applied black whiskers to her face, using her eyeliner and painted on a cute pink nose.

In terms of myself, I had decided to go as Mrs Devil, an outfit also supplied by Jasmine. Unfortunately, this costume was slightly more revealing than hers. Thank goodness I had fairly decent legs because the sequined, red dress I wore was so short in fact that it was practically up to my buttocks. In terms of accessories, I had devil horns and a devil, three-pronged fork, which I attached to my wrist with a thin, red ribbon. Finally, I wore red lipstick and killer black heels, which accentuated my smoky eyes. As I studded myself in the long mirror, I realised that I didn't look like the normal me. I would have quite happily swapped this costume for comfy jeans and a t-shirt any day. Still, it was one night out of the entire year. Therefore, despite my misgivings, I decided to get on with it.

At precisely 7:30pm, Lucifer came to pick up Jasmine and me. When I opened the door, I nearly fell over in shock and delight. Lucifer had dressed up as the devil himself and, in terms of his outfit, he wore a smart, evening suit. He also wore spiky, red horns on his head, a tail, which was peeking out of the tails of his jacket and had a red painted face.

"Wow." I told him, as Jasmine and I took each one of his arms. "Lucifer. You look amazing, although you do slightly remind me of 'Darth Maul' from 'Star Wars'." I added jokingly.

Lucifer smiled.

"Thanks, and so do you." He eventually replied in his deep voice, eyeing up my legs a little too much. "In the end, although we didn't really go as a date, we can still pull off the Mr and Mrs Devil look."

I laughed at his comment although, when I saw Jasmine's awkward expression, I through the spot light onto her instead.

"Jasmine looks far more stunning than me though." I replied and she blushed at my compliment. "She'll knock all the girls here for dead." This comment settled the momentary tense atmosphere, as we all chuckled.

When we entered the dining hall, the three of us gasped in amazement. Gone were the long tables and flags. Now, apart from one table at the back of the hall, which was brimming with food, the entire room was covered in Halloween banners, decorations and candles. Real bats had been let loose and were flying around above our heads, crying to one another and, over in the far side, I nearly had a heart attack when I realised that Miss Beast was in charge of the DJ booth. What's more, she was actually dancing, kind of.

Miss Beast was dressed as a zombie and had really gone to town with her costume, for she was covered in fake blood and wore ripped clothes. As the music blared out of the speakers, playing the latest dance tracks, I realised that perhaps I had misjudged her character and deep down, she was actually a fun person. However, when someone accidently crashed into one of the stands, after dancing vigorously and causing a speaker to wobble, her normal personality returned as she laid into him verbally.

I chuckled and took back my thoughts rapidly.

Lucifer's voice brought me back to reality.

"Hey Alex, do you want to dance?" He suddenly asked me.

I realised that Jasmine had abandoned us and had now gone onto the heaving dance floor with Vince, the boy who had super speed. His date looked very miffed by this situation to say the least.

I nodded.

"Sure." I replied smiling and, for the first time in ages, I let my hair down.

Lucifer and I danced for quite some time and, whilst we did, I had a chance to take in more of my surroundings. First, I noticed that Vladimir (who had dressed up as Frankenstein) was dancing with Mrs Frost, who had come to the Halloween Ball as a grief-stricken, corpse bride. I also noticed that, over in a shadowy corner, Hecate stood softly swaying to the music. She had come as herself, rather to my amusement and was wearing a strikingly beautiful, gossamer, black, gothic lace dress (different to the one she usually wore) and gloves, which really accentuated her pale skin and icy blue eyes. To be fair to her, she looked more gorgeous than ever before.

As I scanned that area, to my surprise, I saw her laugh, actually laugh with a man dressed as a hot-looking 'Dracula'. I was shocked when I realised that the hot 'Dracula' was Mr Allen. Miss Crotchet, who had come as an Egyptian Mummy, was giggling with an older, white-haired man, dressed as a mad scientist, a costume which was very fitting as he was Professor Xandar - the academy's leading Science teacher. Furthermore, I was delighted to see that many of my fellow students had gone all out there with their costumes, for the room was filled with other weird and wonderful creations and creatures such as werewolves, skeletons and exotic aliens (although what these had to do with the theme of Halloween beats me.).

Suddenly, just after a track had finished, I felt a tap on my shoulder. It was Raphael and his face was still as impassive as it had been earlier, after my second rejection.
"Do you mind if I butt in?" He asked Lucifer, who seemed to be startled and a little put out at first, particularly by Raphael's sharp tone and lack of expression.
After a moment's hesitation, Lucifer shrugged and let go of me, for he accepted that he wouldn't be able to steal me forever tonight. "She's all yours." He replied. "However, be careful and I want another dance later."
I nodded.
"I'll book you in." I told him.
Lucifer smiled and moved off to get a drink. When the music started once more, Raphael and I began to move somewhat awkwardly to the beat.
"You look...em...er...beautiful." He abruptly blurted out to my surprise, his eyes trailing over every inch of my body.
I blushed, relieved that he was talking to me. However, deep in his eyes, I thought I still saw a hint of bitterness.
"Thanks." I muttered, feeling slightly out of breath, as I had been dancing for a long time now, before he had showed up. "And you look not bad yourself, although I don't think 'The Joker' is really a Halloween costume, despite the fact that 'Batman' is epic."
Raphael managed a small smile.
"You do have a valid point." He eventually said, shrugging, his golden eyes accentuated even more by the white paint on his face. "But it was the only outfit I could get hold of."
I threw him my famous: 'you must be kidding right?' look.
"There's no way that this was 'the only outfit you could get hold of'." I replied, looking sceptical, although I smiled at him playfully. "My

guess is that your outfit has been hidden away in your case, itching to be worn, knowing just how much of a supervillain geek you are."

Realising that I had caught him out, Raphael's impassive and distant manner vanished. He laughed heartily at my comment. In that moment, I saw just how much he was fighting himself. Finally, he broke free of his previous, coldish manner by meeting my eyes with a longing gaze. This look set my body ablaze.

As our gazes locked, the tension between us broken. I had been such an idiot about not accepting him earlier. As my mind filled with images of Raphael, I realised that the two of us had somehow danced right into the middle of the dining hall. Therefore, I acknowledged, this was the moment when the two main characters of any cheesy romance movie would share a kiss, despite all the drama that had happened in between. To my shock and nervousness, that was exactly what was about to happen.

Immediately, Raphael leaned towards me, his eyes closed and lips slightly parted. Instinctively, I felt myself follow his first move. Just before our lips brushed, I abruptly shouted out in alarm and sharply pulled away. Icy cold liquid hit my heated skin, before it trickled down my sequined dress and chest.

"Oops...I'm so sorry." Vanessa's sarcastic voice sent rage shooting throughout my body, when I had somewhat recovered. She stood smirking at me. "I tripped on something on the floor. I do hope it won't stain?"

It bloody well will stain. I raged internally, as I looked at my costume in despair, which was now soaked in a red, icy drink concoction that resembled blood. *Plus, she had ruined my potentially special moment with Raphael!*

Sick and tired of her torments and fed up with her nasty insults, I faced her leering self, trembling in fury. Vanessa, who was dressed as a sexy vampire, was grinning with her friends, including Tiffany, who wore a matching outfit but in purple. She leered at me. What's more, I noticed that the bruise around her eye had more or less disappeared now, thanks to Mrs Frost's handiwork. However, that wasn't to say that she didn't have room for another one.

As a result of all that she had done, I automatically felt my body burning up with the want to lay into her once more. I wanted to wipe that smirk right off her face. Just before I went to hit her, I remembered my vow to say sorry for my actions. Although this memory pained me, through gritted teeth, I undertook my apology then and there with a sigh.

"You know what Vanessa." I told her in the calmest voice I could muster, despite the fact that I was seething inside, once her gaze had met mine. "I've wanted to apologise for hitting you the other day. It was wrong and I shouldn't have let my anger get the better of me." At hearing these words, Vanessa actually looked surprised and took a step backwards, unable to comprehend what I was saying. Taking a deep breath and feeling Raphael place his hand on my shoulder reassuringly, I continued. "What's more, despite your unfathomable reasons for disliking me and for what you've done, I think that it would be more mature of we put the past behind us." I held out my hand. "Therefore, can we shake on a new beginning, where we can leave each other in peace?"

The look on Vanessa's face, as I spoke, was priceless. It went from utter disbelief, to anger and then, to somewhat understanding. The way she looked at me resembled the way a person might look at an unwanted, filthy, chipped piece of china, before they noticed something quite remarkable and respectful about this item. Nonetheless, she had a reputation at stake. Consequently, with a glance at her followers and admirers, she shook her head.

The fleeting change was gone.

"I don't think that'll ever happen." She retorted, her eyes narrowing to slits. "Especially as I'd never want to touch your hand. You're so far beneath me that physical contact with you would be considered a sin."

For a moment, no one spoke. Even the people around us, who had stopped dancing to stare in shock at what was happening, couldn't believe what they had just heard. I knew that my ears hadn't deceived me. My anger burst from me like a dam, despite Raphael muttering calming words in my ear, as he tried to pull me away. In an instant, I tuned out my senses and let the song of my powers wash over me, filling my entire body with wondrous warmth. It was the fastest time where body and powers became one that anyone, even Vladimir Alcaeus, had witnessed in many years. My eyes shone a dazzling, vibrant blue. Then, I unleashed my power and directed them onto one person and one person only – Vanessa.

Suddenly, Vanessa and I were separated from the others by a powerful wall of water. Vanessa was abruptly picked up by another violent torrent, which streamed from my fingertips and hurtled into an even bigger watery, swirling vortex than the one Jessica Wademen had entered weeks ago. As she entered the gigantic vortex, Vanessa's screams were abruptly cut off, as water soon entered her lungs, causing her to choke and splutter. She desperately pounded against the sides of the vortex, hoping to find a flaw in my handiwork.

All was in vain.

Whilst she stared at me with hazy eyes, I realised that she looked, for the first time, vulnerable. Inside the watery prison, as I controlled the entire situation, I laughed at the sight of her struggling, my eyes flickering crazily. I cheered at the fact that finally, she was getting her fitting end after all she had said and done to me. She deserved every second of it.

Awakening

Vladimir's authoritative voice sounded in my mind.
Let her go! He commanded. *You must let the girl go!*
NO. I shouted back. NO. I'LL NOT 'LET HER GO'. NOT AFTER ALL THE HORRIBLE THINGS SHE'S SAID AND DONE TO ME SINCE WE MET!

In spite of my argument, Vladimir was firm.
That doesn't matter now. He explained, as Vanessa slowly started to get weaker by the second. *If you don't let her go, then she'll die and that's something I'll never allow, nor will you ever forgive yourself for.*
I STILL DON'T CARE! I further argued. SHE'S TORMENTED ME FROM THE START. THEREFORE, SHE SHOULD GET WHAT SHE DESERVES IN THE FORM OF ME AND MY POWERS.

As I raged, I felt an ominous blackness build within my body.
Kill her. Dark thoughts commanded me. *KILL HER!*

Gradually, as this anger flowed throughout my body, much like the time when I almost killed Jessica Wademen, my morals returned. *Don't do this.* They screamed at me. *Don't become a murderer. She's just a silly, immature school girl who, after this, should have learnt her lesson. Listen to Vladimir. He speaks the truth.*
It took a moment for these thoughts to sink in.

With a grunt of tremendous effort, I grabbed hold of my powers and pulled them back within my body. Instantly, the tidal wave collapsed, drenching all who stood nearby and releasing Vanessa from her watery prison. Thankfully, she still had enough strength to stop herself from crashing into the ground for, at the last minute, her powers kicked in, slowing her fall.
Then, she gently fell to the floor in a tight, shaking ball.

After this had happened, I gradually met the terrified gazes of those who had gathered around me. I was consumed with a tremendous dizziness. The room span and my ears rang, but I could see that Jasmine stood nearby, clutching the shoulder of a frightened Lucifer and Raphael looked at me with an expression of both horror, sadness and incredulity.

So much for a "Happy Halloween." I thought sarcastically. *I should wear a huge sign around my neck from now onwards that reads: 'Stay clear of me if you want your party to survive the night'!* With tears streaming down my cheeks, my face bright red and my body trembling, I staggered out of the dining hall and away from the major mess I had caused for the umpteenth time in my life.

CHAPTER 43: ALEX

Blackness clouded my mind. As I ran, the world about me spun. I retched, realising that my powers were too great, at the moment, for my body to cope with. It was Hecate who stopped me from leaving the building, as I reached the front entrance of the academy, skidding to a halt in my black heels.

"Alex!" She cried forcefully, holding out her hand to slow me down, which included blood red fingernails. "Stop running."

I shook my head.

"Let...me...go." I scowled at her, as her cold eyes met mine. I frantically tried to push past her defences. "I don't want to be in this academy for a moment longer."

"You know we can't do that." Another voice joined the two of us, this time it was Mr Allen, who came to a stop next to Hecate, clutching her shoulder, barring my escape for definite. "This is where you belong. This is your second home."

I let out a crazy laugh.

"My second home?" I retorted sarcastically, eyes wild in shock, although I knew that I had once considered his words to be true. "I almost killed a girl just now and yet, you say that this is where I belong and that it's my second home?"

"They both speak the truth." Vladimir's stern voice was the final one to join the throng. I spun around, to meet his serious gaze, heart and head pounding and eyes wide in fear. "You're not to leave this academy until I've given my permission and, up to that point, this place offers protection, support and comfort for all those within its walls."

I suppose that this situation, to you, might appear somewhat comical. I was now officially surrounded by a mysterious, witch woman, a tremendously, hot-looking vampire and an all-powerful, old man dressed as the crazy inventor 'Frankenstein'. I also joined this strange party in my Mrs Devil costume and I felt extremely exposed and embarrassed in my really short outfit. Nonetheless, despite his powerful authority, the craziness of the situation and my lack of clothes, I managed to find my voice.

"But I almost killed a girl." I repeated, trying to place a strong emphasis on this grave fact. "That surely gives you reason to not want me here?"

Vladimir fixed me with a steely gaze.

"We understand the seriousness of what we've just witnessed and acknowledge that your behaviour's cause for concern." Vladimir said, closing the gap between him and me. "However, knowing the strength of your powers, in addition to your potential connection to Mortimer, makes the matter more forgivable. After all," he concluded, "with powers like yours, they're very hard to control should your emotions get the better of you."

At hearing Vladimir's exclamation, I nearly cried. My emotions were all over the place and, to make matters even worse, his statement about this 'Mortimer' person sent shivers up and down my spine.

My heart stopped.

For some reason I couldn't explain, at the sound of Mortimer's name, deep inside of me, something stirred – something monumental.

This something had a huge impact on me.

This something caused me to become even more fearful, especially as I couldn't make sense of the situation.

This something, as crazy and as absurd as it sounds, could be summed up in one word - recognition.

Awakening

Vladimir noticed the change in me instantly. Before anymore could be said on the matter or before I could explode, he sharply gestured for the others to leave the room.

"Please leave us." Vladimir told Hecate and Mr Allen in a firm voice, after he had somewhat recovered, although his eyes were racing with numerous emotions. "And tell no one about what the two of you've just heard."

As soon as Vladimir had spoken, I could tell that Hecate was both surprised and hurt by his dismissal.

Never before had he asked her to leave.

"But Vlad —" Hecate went to argue with him.

Vladimir cut her off with a sharp bark and a flash of his electric, blue eyes.

"I said leave us." His voice was cutting, unlike any tone I had heard him use before.

I swore that I could see Hecate's eyes begin to glisten.

With a frustrated sigh and sharp nod of her head, Hecate turned and left with Mr Allen, using his arm for support.

Now, it was just me and Vladimir Alcaeus.

"Sit." Vladimir told me, gesturing to a chair in the corner. "Sit, for I can tell that you're very weak."

As soon as he had spoken, I did just what he had asked me, without hesitation. My head hurt more than a migraine and I felt battered and bruised internally. An eternity of time seemed to pass before Vladimir spoke once more.

"I can see that my announcement has severely affected you in more ways than one." Vladimir eventually said, his tone steady, which was in complete contradiction to his eyes. "And I can also see that, from your expression, you'd still like nothing better than to run away and leave this place behind. Nevertheless," he continued, "you must understand that I cannot permit that to happen, nor will I allow you to feel the way you do. Therefore," he finalised, "I believe that, in order to help you, I owe you an explanation."

As soon as Vladimir had finished, the world stopped spinning. His words of kindness and reassurance eased my mind a little, in addition to slowing my heartbeat. Therefore, despite my pale face, I permitted myself to reply. By doing so, I began to understand what lay ahead of me.

"M...Mortimer." I exclaimed, finding it terribly hard to say his name for some reason, which unsettled me. "You m...mentioned him. W...who is he?"

At hearing my question, Vladimir didn't answer. Instead, I watched his brow furrow. As it did so, I realised that he was working out how best to tackle the situation. Ultimately, with a small, encouraging smile, he began his tale.

"Many, many years ago, a baby was born. Over the course of time, this baby grew into a boy and then a young man, who eventually had incredible powers. These powers were so amazing in fact that they rivalled my own. However," Vladimir looked forlorn and wistful, remembering old times well before I was delivered onto this planet. "This man was soon corrupted by evil that called to him in the darkness, so much so that he became more malevolent than any of us could possibly imagine, until it was almost too late to stop him."

Vladimir paused for a moment to collect his thoughts.
Then, he continued.
"Mortimer," Vladimir grew distant again and his eyes became misty with remembrance. "Now immortal and incised with rage and jealousy, gradually grew stronger as the years went by. What's more, he began to collect together an invincible army, unbeknownst to me, both made up of the living and the dead." Vladimir shivered. "Not long after his followers had been united, an almighty battle took place between his kind and our own. We fought for what felt like an

eternity, losing many on both sides along the way. Then, in the last moments, which I had thought was lost on my part, I managed to defeat Mortimer and imprison him in a dimension far away from here." Suddenly, Vladimir looked at me with a haunted expression. "Despite all that, in present times, Mortimer's re-awoken and is planning to return to Earth to wreak his revenge on all those who wronged him, including me. That's why he must be stopped, somehow, once and for all."

Now, whilst Vladimir had been talking, the candles flickered threateningly all around us. This feeling deep inside me, this feeling of recognition, also became more disturbingly stronger the longer Vladimir spoke. Consequently, this lead me to enquire further about my supposed 'connection' to this tyrant.

As I did so, my voice became filled with terror.

"You said earlier that I'm 'connected' to Mortimer?" I cried, feeling my heart rate increase considerably in my panic. "However, I've never even heard of this man, let alone seen him."

At hearing my emotional outburst, Vladimir's features softened and he took my hand in his. I felt the strength of his own tremendous powers coincide with mine.

"I understand what you're saying and, to be honest, I still find that part of the situation a mystery. Nevertheless," he continued, "when I saw your powers a moment ago, as you created that huge, water wall and vortex, I know and so does Hecate that we're right in our suspicions. This conformation also helped by the fact that Hecate's been keeping an eye on you for many days now and has reported back to me with information concerning your talent and nature!"

So that was why Hecate was constantly popping up whenever I was around? At least that made more sense now and I was relieved to think that she was clearly not some kind of stalker, even though she was still pretty odd. All this information was so overwhelming. Eventually, I asked the question that both of us were now thinking.

"H...how do we stop M...Mortimer?" I stammered, petrified. My stomach rocketed so much that I thought I'd be violently sick all over Vladimir's ancient, expensive carpet.

For the last time that night, Vladimir looked at me in both sympathy and sorrow. We had a similar idea with regards to the matter — an idea that terrified me more than you could possibly know and, as Vladimir turned my suspicions into a reality, it took so much effort not to scream.

"Truthfully," Vladimir clarified, "Hecate and I are still unsure about how we can put an end to Mortimer, once and for all. Nevertheless," he added, "as a result of your apparent 'connection', both of us believe that you're to play a strong part in this matter. All the same," he concluded, "whether you undertake this task alone is another matter best decided in the near future."

As soon as Vladimir had revealed all, I wanted the ground to swallow me up. If I was linked to Mortimer somehow then, from this moment onwards, I had to make it my main goal to locate Mortimer and destroy him, before he obliterated me and everyone that I loved. Such a happy thought! However, was this what I wanted, or was this all some part of an ancient, long-woven plan?

"W...what if I said no t...to all of this?" I suddenly exclaimed, eyes filled with fear at the enormity of the situation. "What if I said that I don't want anything to do with Mortimer?"

At hearing my defiant answer, Vladimir looked at me with an unreadable expression.

An age seemed to pass before he spoke.

"Then that would be your choice." He eventually stated. "No one's forcing you to go through with this task. Instead," he added, "people, like me, are just guiding you and acting upon their own beliefs, morals and opinions. At the end of the day," he continued, "although many believe in fate, it's those who go through life with independent thought alone who are the strongest. Furthermore," he concluded, "although we're all connected to one another somehow, sometimes for reasons beyond our knowledge, it's how we take control of these connections, using our free will to define our actions and the following consequences."

When Vladimir had finished talking, all I could do was sit there in awe. With this concluding speech, Vladimir had summed up the pinnacle of how I was presently feeling. Deciding what must be done, for now at least, I made my oath. I spoke in the steadiest voice I could conjure and hoped that I was making the right decision – a decision that was made by me and not anyone else.

"I, Alexandra Raven, daughter of Cathy and Toby Raven and great grand-daughter of the legendary Alistair Silverstone, pledge my word to accept whatever role I am to play and vow to do my best in bringing down Mortimer and all who follow him."

And so, from that moment onwards, my battle against evil truly began...

EPILOGUE

*D*eep in the hottest, blackest and evilest part of Darkvoid dimension, Mortimer was roused from his malevolent dreams by the sound of tormented crying, filled with pain. As he awoke, he cursed the one who had disturbed his slumber, with red eyes flashing in fury. Then, in a swirl of silver mist, he lost his original form and took the appearance of a remarkably handsome, young man with pale, almost translucent skin, coal eyes and raven hair. His clothes were the colour of the moon and he had small crystal diamonds in the shape of skulls on his sleeves.

As Mortimer studded his unusual handsomeness in the mirror before him, which he had just conjured out of thin air with lethargic ease, he smiled at himself, displaying a set of perfectly straight, white teeth. Boy did he love being the most powerful being the entire world!

Almost the most powerful being in the entire world. You're forgetting the one person who was able to outshine your talents all those countless years ago, which ensured that you became entangled in this foul imprisonment.

At this infuriating thought, Mortimer growled menacingly and clenched his fists so hard that his long, thin nails bit into his flesh, drawing blood.

"Not for long though!" He sharply muttered, underneath his breath. "Soon, if all goes to plan, I'll hold that title and many others in the near future and my old foe, Vladimir Achilles Alcaeus," Mortimer said triumphantly, his eyes flashing. "Will be no more." With another swirl of mist, he glided down the fiery steps of his trapped tomb and into the grand chamber he had created using nothing but dark powers and a twisted imagination. Subsequently, he came to stand in front of the wretched creature responsible for waking him from his slumber.

Rather than filled with anger at this fact, Mortimer's black heart became filled with glee, as he studied the broken man before him. He realised that the first phase of his plan was hopefully about to become a glorious reality and it all started with this unfortunate victim. Still, he realised gloomily, that was only if his loyal servants had succeeded in their task which, unfortunately from past experiences, was an infrequent occurrence.

"So, you're the next individual my servants have decided to bring to me, in order for my master plan to finally begin?" He sneered, giving the battered man a poke with his pointed nail. He circled the human with distain, waving off his misgivings for now. Once he had completed two whole circles, he lifted his finger up to his mouth, which was now smeared with congealed blood and tasted it, sighing in pleasure. As Mortimer smacked his lips in delight, blood tingling in his mouth, he saw the man shiver with revulsion and terror at this act. Inside, Mortimer bubbled in excitement. If he wanted the best possible outcome for what he was about to do, then maximum fear was necessary. "I do hope you won't disappoint me." Mortimer continued, once more circling his dejected victim and frowning in displeasure at the thought of something going wrong. "Otherwise, I'll be very angry indeed and," he paused dramatically, before resuming his speech. "When I'm angry, things get extremely unpleasant. We wouldn't want that now...would we?"

When Mortimer had finished, he stopped in front of the man, before bursting out into a cold, mocking laugh that rang about the entire prison. This laugh caused dark beings, hiding just out of sight, to scuttle away in alarm. When he finished laughing, Mortimer resumed his business demeanour almost immediately, with scary control.

"Pain, Suffering!" Mortimer snapped, making his prey jump at the sharpness of his tone. "Where are you?"

Immediately, Mortimer's eyes flashed red, until they turned back into their normal deathly colour when his demon servants answered his call.

"Ssssire?" Suffering abruptly hissed, appearing out of thin air, his fiery body aglow with heat and the stench of burning flesh filling the chamber, causing the prisoner to retch violently in disgust.

"You called ussss?" Pain added, his shaking body pale and weak and giving off the repulsive odour of decay.

Despite seeing the clear discomfort of his broken quarry, Mortimer seemed indifferent to the nauseating smell of both his servants, for he just fixed them with a hostile stare once they had arrived.

"Yes." Mortimer snarled in a voice that was icy and harsh. "I called you because I wanted to make sure that this human will definitely fit the criteria needed to begin my master plan. I do not want a repeat performance of what happened last time." Mortimer shuddered in angry remembrance. "That previous victim – Joseph Cunnings - was hardly deemed innocent. After the ritual had failed, it was evident that he was high up on the 'sinning scale'. What's more," he added, "despite the fact I've tasted this being's blood and it seems fine, if you get your task wrong again, I'll make sure that you both suffer even more than you did before. Do you understand?"

After Mortimer had finished his frosty and cutting accusation, he noticed how both his servants gulped in unease, before they rubbed their heads in remembrance of some form of horrid punishment. They had deserved it. In his mind, they reminded him of 'Tweedledee' and 'Tweedledum', with an extra emphasis placed on the 'dum'!

Bravely, Pain spoke.

"Of coursssse, sssire." Pain said, his voice now as shaky as his body. Mortimer saw Suffering nod his head in agreement.

"We underssstand and we promisse that we've got it right thiss time. We doubled and tripled checked the criteria before bringing him here. Honesst."

After Pain had replied, Mortimer stared hard into his eyes, scanning those watery, agony filled depths. Soon, he sighed, relieved. For the final time, in relation to his current circumstances, he would place his trust in his most devoted servants.

"Very well." Mortimer barked, his eyes flashing in cold acceptance. "But," he added, looking at Pain and Suffering fiercely in turn. "Don't let me down again! Otherwise, you'll feel the full extent of my wrath." Subsequently, he turned his full attention to his prisoner, who had unfortunately been conscious enough to overhear the whole conversation beneath matted and filthy hair.

Realising that something terrible was about to happen to him, the man spoke for the first time, looking at Mortimer directly in the eye.

"P...please let...le...t me go." He cried, his eyes filled with dread, anguish and panic. He tried feebly to wrench out of the chains that bound him to the chamber floor. "I don...don't know where this is, b...but I demand that y...you take me back home...at...at once."

After he had finished his passionate plea, Mortimer exchanged looks with Pain and Suffering. Then, all three burst out laughing. At hearing this amusing statement, Mortimer laughed so much that he actually cried hot fiery tears, which fell from his black eyes and burned holes in the chamber floor. Pain and Suffering also let out cries of wheezy laughter, spraying their captive with even more foul fumes. Choking and spluttering, the trapped man fixed Mortimer with another terrified stare.

Watching the flaming tears fall down his cheeks, he let out a cry of alarm.

"Are...are yo...you the dev...devil?" He suddenly stammered, shaking with dread and eyes wide in fear. "And is...is th...is h...h...hell?"

As soon as the words had left his lips, they only made Mortimer laugh even harder, causing sparks of phenomenal power to fly from his fingertips. Eventually, still chuckling in amusement, Mortimer responded to his hostage's plea and questions.

"I have to give it to you two." He said, grinning at Pain and Suffering for the first time in an age, who smiled back at him, relieved that their master was in such a good mood. "You certainly caught a very amusing soul here." Straitening his tie and wiping his eyes on a black hanky, which disintegrated as a result of his heated tears, Mortimer spoke, his voice now deadly serious. "However, before I answer your questions and, although you've caused me great amusement, I want complete and utter SILENCE from you." He snapped, his tone filled with contempt and control.

Instantly, snapping his long fingers, the man found that he was unable to talk for, although his mouth continued to move in protest, no sound came out, much to his utter shock and terror. As he desperately clutched at his throat in alarm, his chains rattling, Mortimer smiled wickedly, before he continued to speak.

"That's better." He grinned, when his victim finally admitted defeat. "Although, when we begin the ritual, which will be very soon I assure you, I want to hear your vocal chords sing like they've never sung before." Mortimer threw Pain and Suffering a knowing smile. They chuckled coldly at the man's terrified gaze. "Nevertheless," Mortimer continued, flashing his prisoner a dazzling smile. "Before all that happens, I'll grant you the answers to your very amusing plea and questions."

Mortimer paused for a moment, to collect his thoughts.

Awakening

Then, he revealed all.

"As for your demand to make us take you home...that'll have to be sadly rejected." Mortimer pouted. "Even if we did let you go, which would never happen, you would find that there would be no home for you to return to anyway." Mortimer grinned coldly. "My loyal servants saw to that before they came back to me bearing you."

At this comment, Mortimer's eyes flashed in cold delight. He bathed in the thought of such beautiful destruction and the look of complete shock and grief that fell over his captive's features. Pain and Suffering exchanged malicious glances. All the same, Mortimer was not finished.

"Moving swiftly on, as for your questions about I being the devil and this being hell, they have very interesting answers."

When Mortimer spoke, he seemed to grow taller and the darkness in the room intensified. Furthermore, he positioned himself directly in front of the trembling human, so that their faces were almost touching. Then, he whispered something into his ear, which caused his prey to feel the worst fear he had and would ever experience. He cried out in alarm.

"This is my version of hell and, although the Devil and I are acquaintances, I'm far worse than he ever deemed was possible." Mortimer hissed before, not giving the ensnared man any chance to reply, he plunged his fist into his chest, releasing him from the non-talking charm and ripping out his still beating heart.

The sound of his prisoner's screams of agony was like music to Mortimer's ears, whilst his vivid, red blood flowed freely down his chest. What's more, Mortimer laughed in joy, as the blood gushed down his arms, staining his silver suit forever. Still, he didn't worry about that. He would just conjure up another one when the wonderful deed was done. In a matter of seconds, the man disintegrated before Mortimer, consumed by a raging ball of fire, until he was nothing but ashes. Mortimer didn't even bat an eyelid at this fact. Instead, he was far more interested in the beating heart he held close to his chest which, much to his delight, illuminated his face in a golden hue. This heart told him that he had succeeded in starting his long-desired plan.

As Pain and Suffering celebrated around him, Mortimer knew that there was one thing left to do, in order to finalise this first stage. Bringing the glowing heart close to his mouth, he tore into it with animalistic and frenzied intent. Eventually, the last gleaming morsel had been consumed. As he felt the change within him and heard the sound of an almighty barrier being torn, which was ear-splittingly loud, Mortimer bellowed in joy.

His eyes became redder than ever before.

Once the first stage had been completed and Mortimer was able to stare across the heavens and see Earth in the near distance, he allowed himself to rejoice in the festivities, alongside Pain and Suffering and the rest of his dead companions. Two parts of his plan remained until he would once again be able to wreak his revenge. Furthermore, this time, Mortimer smiled knowingly, as he drunk a whole glass of blood in one go, Vladimir Alcaeus, that meddlesome witch Hecate and the girl Alexandra Raven – who he had recently found out about from his servants - would not put an end to his ultimate plan. Consequently, Mortimer joined in the festivities, with glorious victory residing deep within his blackened heart and cold eyes once more aglow with a sinister fire.

A SHORT ACKNOWLEDGEMENT

    I would like to take the opportunity to say thank you to the one person in my life who means more to me than words could ever express – *my mother*. She is and will always be my rock, my best friend, my guide and my guardian angel. She showed me that I should never give up on my dreams or let life grind me down and, without her patience, her unwavering love and complete support, I would not be where or who I am today. She will *forever* hold a special place in my heart and the bond that we share will *never* be broken, no matter what. She is an inspiration and I am proud to call you my mother. I will love you unconditionally, until the end of time.

Us two together, forever and always!

XXXXXXXXX